A WHEELER PARK CHRISTMAS

THE WITCHES OF WHEELER PARK: BOOK 5

CHRISTINE POPE

Dark Valentine Press

This is a work of fiction. Names, characters, places, and incidents are either the product of the author's imagination or are used fictitiously. Any resemblance to actual events, places, organizations, or persons, whether living or dead, is entirely coincidental.

A WHEELER PARK CHRISTMAS

ISBN: 978-1-946435-38-5

Published by Dark Valentine Press

Cover design by Lou Harper/Cover Affairs

Ebook formatting by Indie Author Services

Addie Grant

"I DON'T THINK THE WEATHER IS GOING TO change just because you keep staring out the window," Jake teased me, and I turned away from the window in question and gave him a wry smile.

"Probably not," I replied.

Of course, the joke was that, under normal circumstances, I probably could have changed the weather if I'd wanted to. That was my talent, after all—controlling the weather, summoning storms and rain, even using lightning as a weapon if I had no other choice.

Problem was, even I needed something to work with, and the skies over Flagstaff had been blindingly, achingly clear for the entire month of

December. I could push clouds from one place to another as long as they weren't too far away, but with the nearest storms way off in the Pacific Northwest, there didn't seem to be much of anything even my particular magical gift could do to change the current situation in my adopted hometown.

"Look at it this way," he said. "At least you don't have to go tromping through snow drifts to do your Christmas shopping."

That was Jake—always trying to see the bright side of any given situation. In this particular case, though, I had to admit he had a point. I'd had to cram all my shopping into the few days between the end of the fall semester and Christmas Eve, now only four days off, and the task would have been a lot more difficult to manage if I'd been trudging through the snow to buy all those presents.

Being so extravagant for Christmas was definitely a new experience for me. Growing up, I'd never had much money. But my recent entry into the Wilcox clan had also been accompanied by a large inheritance from my birth father, a man I'd never met but who had once been in charge of the whole family. The inheritance I'd received was so enormous, I still didn't quite know what to do with it.

So, I'd gone Christmas shopping. Presents for

Jake, of course, and for his younger brother Jeremy and his girlfriend Sloane. And for Jake and Jeremy's parents, Raymond and Theresa, and for my half-brother Connor and his wife Angela and the nieces and nephew I hadn't even known I had until the past summer. The joy of being able to shop however I liked had been shadowed by the knowledge I wouldn't be able to share the holiday with my mother, but I'd promised myself that I would do my best to let the sorrow go and concentrate on my current happiness.

All the presents I'd purchased were now piled under the enormous Christmas tree that took pride of place in the living room of the big Victorian house Jake and I shared. Looking at all those brightly wrapped presents and festive gift bags, I wondered if I'd gone a little overboard.

But hey, it was my first Christmas with my new family, and with Jake. I supposed I'd be forgiven for being just a wee bit extravagant.

If only it would snow.

Jake came over to the window and wrapped his arms around me. I snuggled against his shoulder, breathing in the warm scent of his skin and the woodsy aroma that always seemed to drift from his thick, dark hair. "It does this sometimes," he said, his voice a warm murmur at my ear. "We'll get one storm to tease us, and then it's clear for weeks. Our heaviest snowfalls come in January and February."

Which I knew was only the truth, since I'd looked up records of snowfall amounts in the Flagstaff area, just to reassure myself that this sort of cold, dry weather wasn't all that unusual. Still, I'd really wanted my first Christmas with my new family to be a white one, just because my vision of an ideal holiday included snowy winter landscapes and soft flakes drifting down outside the windows of my house. I'd had visions of the San Francisco Peaks crowned with snow, of the streets in the city's pretty downtown area coated with a blanket of white.

And okay, there actually was some snow on Mt. Humphreys and the other mountains that towered above the town, just because we'd had a storm right before Thanksgiving that dumped nearly a foot in the lower elevations and almost twice that much on the peaks themselves. It hadn't warmed up enough for the snow to melt all the way, so it wasn't as if the mountains were bare rock. Still....

"Maybe if we all thought good thoughts," I said, only halfway joking, and he kissed the side of my neck, sending a delicious thrill through my body. You'd think after living with him for almost six months, I'd be a little more used to his presence, but that didn't seem to be the case. My pulse still sped up every time he touched me, and it was probably a good thing that I'd had such a heavy academic load the past semester. Otherwise, the two of us would have spent way too much time in bed.

"Good thoughts are always appreciated," he replied. Although he stood behind me and I couldn't really see his expression, I had a feeling he was smiling, brown eyes showing their usual crinkles of amusement, handsome features lit up with affection. "Anyway, we need to head out, or we're going to be late."

"Right." I closed the blinds, and Jake stepped away from me and went and performed the same task with the window coverings on the other side of the room. The rest of the house had already been closed up—dusk came early at this time of year—but I'd left the living room blinds open so I could look outside on the off chance that the weather might suddenly change.

No such luck, though, and I supposed it was just as well. The house Jake and I shared was only a few blocks away from our cousin Laurel's apartment in downtown Flagstaff, and since the weather appeared to be holding, we'd planned to walk over there rather than fight for parking. Temperatures would be bitterly cold, well below freezing, but I'd bought myself a couple of good coats and accompanying scarves and gloves and hats, so I figured I'd survive the walk.

Jake and I suited up, and I wound a plaid cashmere scarf around my throat as he jammed a knit cap down on his head, smashing his dark brown hair.

"You're going to have hat hair," I warned him, and he grinned.

"I'm not trying to impress anybody."

No, probably not, since almost everyone at Laurel's party would be a Wilcox, with maybe a sprinkling of McAllisters who'd decided to make the drive to Flag for the evening. Why she was even throwing a solstice party, I didn't know for sure; the Wilcoxes weren't practicing pagans like the McAllister clan. Most likely, Laurel had gotten the idea from something she'd seen on Instagram or Twitter.

But after keeping my head down all semester and working my ass off so I wouldn't be too behind after switching majors, I wanted a party just as badly as anyone else. The reason behind it didn't matter so much. And it should be pretty informal, since Laurel had only invited those of her cousins who were around our age or a little younger, all the twenty-somethings who weren't yet married and starting families.

I wasn't sure I really wanted to think about that, however. Not that I had any interest in having kids yet—I had way too much schoolwork ahead of me—but Jake and I had been living together since the end of June, and he hadn't yet said one word about getting married. Maybe he assumed I wanted to wait on making things formal until after I graduated, and yet…

…and yet, I really wished he would ask, if only to make things feel a bit more settled between the two of us. I couldn't imagine my world without him…didn't want to imagine a life that didn't have Jake Wilcox in it. I loved him no matter what, but I also found myself wondering what he was waiting for.

But we were on our way to a party, and I certainly didn't want to be brooding over such a fraught topic. As best I could, I pushed my worries to the back of my mind, following Jake outside so we could head down the front steps and start making our way to Laurel's place.

The raw night air bit my face almost as soon as we hit the sidewalk, but I was used to it. Honestly, Flagstaff really wasn't much colder than some of the places I'd lived in Wyoming and Colorado, and by this point, I'd become accustomed to the chilly weather.

Jake's gloved hand stole into mine, and I wrapped my fingers around his, glad of the steadiness of his grip. Since no snow had fallen for weeks, I didn't have to worry about ice so much, but there were still places where the sidewalks were less than even, and it helped to have him to hold on to as we walked in the darkness.

Then again, I probably would have been just as thrilled to have his hand in mine if the sidewalks had been perfectly smooth and we'd been walking in blazing daylight.

Neither of us spoke, which was fine. I liked it that Jake didn't see the need to fill silence with chatter, that he was comfortable enough in my company that we could simply be quiet and enjoy being with each other.

Besides, it was probably going to be plenty loud where we were going.

My suspicions were confirmed when we reached Laurel's building and began climbing the stairs to her loft apartment. Down below was an art gallery that Connor owned in addition to the loft Laurel was renting, along with a coffee bar that had been a recent acquisition when the previous business, an outdoor supply company, folded and closed up shop. As we got closer to the door of her apartment, the sound of a pounding bass line greeted us, overlaid with the babble of what sounded like dozens of voices.

Inwardly, I quailed a bit. Over the past six months, I'd met a good number of my Wilcox cousins, but by no means all of them. I still couldn't help experiencing butterflies in my stomach at the thought of having to face a whole batch of people who were strangers to me, although I told myself to suck it up. Whoever was in there, either they were actual relatives or, in the case of any McAllister witches and warlocks who'd come up to Flagstaff for the party, at least still witch-kind. Laurel had told me that she didn't plan to invite any civilians to her solstice get-together.

"I mean, it's not like I don't have civilian friends," she'd said quickly after making that confession. We'd been sitting at the coffee bar downstairs with Jeremy's girlfriend Sloane, having a cup while the guys were off doing their Christmas shopping—presumably for our presents, since they hadn't wanted us anywhere around them. "But it's so much easier when we don't have to watch everything we say, you know?"

Sloane and I had both nodded. She was a gorgeous girl who was about a million times more sophisticated than I could ever hope to be, but we had one thing in common—we were both "orphan" witches who'd been raised outside our clans, and so we'd experienced very recently how difficult it could be sometimes to make sure not a single betraying syllable about the witching world escaped our lips when civilians were around.

At any rate, I knew I wouldn't have to worry about guarding my tongue at Laurel's party. As for the rest—well, I'd survived meeting dozens of Wilcox relatives so far. A few more couldn't hurt.

A wall of sound greeted us as soon as Jake opened the door. I tried not to wince, but I had a feeling I didn't entirely succeed, judging by the quick flash of a grin I spotted on his lips. Without saying anything, he led me over to the coat rack near the door so we could take off our puffer jackets and scarves and hats. As soon as he pulled off the knit cap he wore, he ran a quick hand through his hair and then sent me another grin, as if to show that my worry about possible "hat hair" had been completely unfounded.

I glanced around, looking for Laurel. No sign of her at first, which wasn't all that surprising, considering it seemed to be wall-to-wall people inside her loft apartment. It felt to me as though she had to be violating at least a couple fire codes, but I supposed that wasn't as big a problem when you had a crowd of witches and warlocks. Surely one of them had a skill that could be put to use extinguishing fires.

Just as my own talent with the weather had come in handy when I'd used it to put out a prairie fire in Wyoming the summer before. Of course, back then, I hadn't thought it was quite so handy, considering my weather gifts had led Agent Randall Lenz, former head of Homeland Security's Project Daedalus, right to my front door. In the end, though, everything had worked out. After all, if he hadn't caught me, I would never been able to prove to him that he actually was a warlock...and he would never have made the decision to help free all the witches and warlocks he was holding at the facility he managed in Virginia.

That one good deed couldn't quite erase every-thing else he'd done. He'd sworn that his gun had discharged accidentally when he'd come to collect me from my mother's house in Kanab, but his protestations couldn't alter the fact that it was a bullet from his gun which had killed her.

Needless to say, Randall Lenz and I weren't exactly best friends. Connor had given him shelter in Flagstaff, since he'd left Homeland Security in disgrace, and it had seemed like the right thing to do at the time. Even so, I could only be glad the town was big enough that we could do a pretty good job of avoiding each other.

And I certainly didn't have to worry about him being at Laurel's party. For one thing, no one there was over thirty, and for another, he wouldn't have come even if she had invited him. As far as I could tell, Randall Lenz had been keeping a very low profile lately.

"Addie!"

I turned at the sound of Laurel's voice, a smile on my lips to match the one she was wearing. She headed over toward me, red Solo cup in one hand, amber-brown eyes looking bigger than ever thanks to the false eyelashes she'd put on for the party, her long brown hair falling in loose waves. From the way she teetered in her high-heeled boots, it looked as though she had already consumed at least one drink.

Before I could move, she'd thrown her arms around me. "Happy solstice!"

"Happy solstice," I responded as I returned the hug, since I didn't know what else to say.

"Happy solstice, Laurel," Jake remarked, tone just a bit too ironic. "Good thing you're not driving."

That comment made her raise an eyebrow. "Please. This is only my second beer. I just shouldn't have worn these boots tonight—I'm still breaking them in."

"Whatever you say."

She disentangled her arms from me and took an ostentatious swallow of beer. "Anyway, the booze and the food are all over in the dining area, so help yourself. I know Sloane and Jeremy are here somewhere, but I haven't seen them for a couple of minutes."

Which didn't surprise me, considering how packed the place was. I nodded, and Laurel wandered off, apparently content to let us make our own introductions to any strangers we encountered. Not that there seemed to be that many—I recognized lots of Wilcox cousins, and smiled and did sort of awkward half-waves at them as Jake and I made our way over to the refreshment table.

Or tables, actually, since Laurel had all the drinks set out on a small sideboard and the actual food was on the dining room table. Real food, too —a plate of sandwiches she must have gotten from a local deli, potato and pasta salad, and a platter of raw veggies and dip in addition to several kinds of chips and a big plate of cookies.

She had wine and glasses set out on the drinks table, along with mixers and some hard stuff. I got a cup of wine while Jake poured himself some beer from the keg she'd stashed in the corner, some kind of lager from a local brewery instead of a national brand.

"I didn't know Laurel got so elaborate with her parties," I said as Jake and I found ourselves a spot off to one side where we wouldn't get crushed by people looking for booze or food. "Does she do this a lot?"

"First time," he replied. "I mean, she's had some smaller parties here since she moved in a while back, but she's never done this solstice thing before. I think she's just looking for stuff to keep her occupied."

I nodded. Considering that Trident Enterprises—Jake's witch-finding operation in Wheeler Park—had basically been turning up goose eggs ever since Jeremy found Sloane back in September, I could see why Laurel was doing what she could to stay busy. And their ongoing inaction certainly wasn't for lack of trying. Every day, Jake and Jeremy and Laurel went to the renovated house they used as their base of operations and did everything they could to track down their next "orphaned" witch or warlock. But either there just weren't as many of them out there as they'd thought, or the ones still circulating in regular society were way better at hiding themselves than I had been.

"Sorry things have been such crap for you lately," I said, and Jake shrugged.

"It'll turn around," he said. "We all knew that having big gaps in our 'rescues' might happen. Just part of the territory. Jeremy and I have been keeping busier because we're turning one of the upstairs bedrooms into a meeting room, but until he and I are done with the carpentry work and the wiring and we're ready to paint the place, Laurel doesn't have much to do."

Yes, the two brothers had decided to tackle that project about a month earlier. It was definitely plenty of work for the two of them—I was still kind of boggled that they had the skill set to take on that particular task—but it was also the kind of thing they could do while Jeremy's algorithms were running in the background, searching for any clan-less witches or warlocks who might be out there somewhere.

I was about to reply when Jake's cousin Jasper came over to us. We'd met once in passing at the Trident Enterprises house, and I still couldn't quite figure him out. He was around Jake's age, maybe a year or so older, quiet and intense, with shoulder-length black hair he sometimes wore back in a ponytail and impressive sleeves of tattoos on both arms. Those tattoos weren't visible at the moment, since he was wearing a black hoodie, but I still knew they were there.

His talent was creating undetectable illusions that would last forever. Only on inanimate objects, though—he couldn't change his own appearance or that of anyone else, but he could make a plain piece of plastic look like an Arizona driver's license, as he'd done for me after I fled Utah without my purse and any form of identification. Eventually, I'd taken a birth certificate he'd cooked up for me and gotten myself a real license with my real name on it, but still, if it hadn't been for him, I would have had a much more difficult time starting over.

"Hey," he said, nodding at both Jake and me as he held a red cup identical to the one Laurel had been drinking out of.

"Hey," we replied, almost in unison.

"What's up?" Jake continued. Obviously, he thought there had to be a reason why Jasper had approached us, since he generally didn't seem to be the type who volunteered much. People approached Jasper Wilcox and not the other way around, which was why it seemed a little strange that he would have come over to Jake and me almost as soon as we got to the party. Then again, I hadn't really been able to figure him out yet, so trying to decipher his motivations tended to be an exercise in futility.

Jasper ran a hand through his hair, pushing it back away from his face so he could tuck some of the heavy strands behind one ear. "Joanna wants to talk to you."

"Joanna?" I repeated, giving a quick look around the packed apartment. It really didn't seem like her kind of scene, but because it was so crowded, I supposed she could have been in there somewhere.

"She's not here," Jasper said. He looked almost amused—or at least, I assumed that faint lift of one eyebrow meant he thought it was funny that I'd thought the no-nonsense Joanna, the Wilcox clan's other weather-worker, would be attending Laurel's kegger.

"If she wanted to talk to Addie, why didn't she call?" Jake asked, which seemed like a perfectly logical question to me. It wasn't that Joanna and I were besties or anything—she was five or six years older than I, and in a completely different place in her life—but we still talked occasionally if I had a question about a particular aspect of weather control or something like that.

Jasper shrugged. "I was over at her place helping her mend one of her fences, and I mentioned that I was going to be at the party tonight. That's when she told me to let you know she wanted to talk."

"Did she say about what?" I said.

"No. I didn't ask. Joanna's not the type to invite a lot of poking and prying."

I couldn't argue with that statement. She always seemed fairly private, although I supposed my impressions of her could have been formed mostly from our differences in personality and nothing else.

"Well, it can't be an emergency, or she would have called you," Jake said reasonably.

True. Jasper seemed to be in agreement with that observation, because he gave another lift of his shoulders and said, "Yeah, probably. Anyway, just wanted to pass that on before I forgot."

He ambled off, cup still clutched in one hand. I had to hope he still had plenty of beer or whatever he'd been drinking, since he hadn't made a move to replenish it while he was over by the drinks table.

Jake watched him, brows pulling together in a small frown. "That was weird."

"Was it?" I asked, then sipped some of my merlot. It wasn't great, but it was decent enough for party drinking. "No offense, but everything about Jasper seems a little weird."

That observation earned me a chuckle. "Nah, Jasper's okay. I mean, he keeps to himself, but we can't all be party animals, right?"

I arched an eyebrow at him. "I wasn't aware that we were party animals."

"Compared to Jasper, we are."

Since Jake's comment was nothing more than the truth, I had to grin up at him. Yes, we didn't go out every night because I was carrying twenty-four units a semester at Northern Pines University, trying to get caught up with my English lit requirements without having to go another semester or possibly a whole year, but that didn't mean we didn't have any kind of social life. We went to the movies and out to dinner, to gallery openings and programs at Lowell Observatory, went hiking and did day trips to Jerome and Winslow and the Grand Canyon.

"Well, let's go party, you animal," I said, still smiling. "I'll call Joanna in the morning and find out what she wants."

"Deal," Jake replied.

Another swallow of wine, and I thought I might be brave enough to meet the rest of the gang.

Maybe.

2

Jake Wilcox

HE SAT ON THE BED, TURNING THE SMALL ring box over and over in his hand. It was safe to pull it out and look at it, because Addie had just stepped into the shower and probably wouldn't be out for at least fifteen or twenty minutes. Her showers always took longer on the days when she washed her hair.

Although she'd remained silent on the topic, he knew she'd begun to wonder why he hadn't done or said anything to make their relationship more formal. Back in Wyoming when he'd told her he'd make a home wherever she was, no matter where that might be, he'd hinted at marriage, even though at that point, it had been far too early in their relationship for him to have actually asked the fateful question.

But now it was six months later, and it seemed clear enough to both of them—and to the rest of the clan, probably—that their relationship was one that would last. However, Addie had been so busy with school that Jake hadn't wanted to do anything to distract her.

The holidays seemed like the perfect opportunity, though. She wouldn't be back at school until after the first of the year, and that would give them the time they needed to start planning. A Christmas Eve proposal, he'd thought, there in the living room with the lights on the big Noble fir glittering in the background and a fire in the hearth giving a warm glow to everything. Snow falling beyond the windows with their stained-glass borders, creating a picture-perfect backdrop for his proposal.

Too bad there didn't seem to be much chance of a white Christmas that year.

It wasn't important. What mattered was giving the ring to Addie and letting her know that he hadn't forgotten her, wasn't having second thoughts. No, he'd only wanted to wait for the perfect moment.

He opened the box and stared down at the ring inside. As soon as he started shopping for a diamond, he'd realized selecting the right one was going to be harder than he'd thought. Nothing ostentatious or fussy, because Addie wasn't much into frills. And even though he could afford to get her something big and expensive, he guessed she wouldn't be on board with that, either. Neither of them had any need to be frugal, but she still studied all the sales flyers from the local grocery stores carefully and made up their shopping lists based on whatever was on special, still went directly to the sales rack when clothes shopping and rarely—if ever—paid full price for anything.

But this ring…as soon as he saw it, he knew it was the right one for her. A special square cut called an Asscher, with extra facets to make it sparkle. Just a little over a carat, enough to show up on her hand without being too showy. No extra stones, only a simple platinum setting to showcase the stone it held.

From the bathroom came the sound of the shower door sliding open, and Jake hastily closed the ring box and went to stuff it in the catch-all drawer of his nightstand. He knew Addie would never look in there; the jumble of loose change and old keychains and receipts and other papers was definitely enough to ensure she'd stay away.

She didn't come out into the bedroom, but stayed in the master bath, humming under her breath as she got to work blow-drying her hair. Although the sound of a blow dryer wasn't generally the most euphonious thing in the world, Jake liked to hear it, liked to think of her only a few feet away, getting ready to start their day.

Which in this particular case meant heading over to his cousin Joanna's house once Addie was ready. She'd texted Joanna earlier that morning, letting her know that Jasper had passed along word that Joanna wanted to see Addie. Joanna had responded by saying they could come by that morning, and so they'd accelerated their preparations slightly, since their original plan had been to pretty much laze around the house and watch holiday shows on Netflix or something now that they had all their Christmas shopping done.

Joanna hadn't let slip anything of why she wanted to see Addie, but since his cousin tended to hold her cards pretty close to her vest, Jake didn't find her reticence all that surprising. If it was something they could handle over the phone, she would have told Addie as much.

"I'll meet you downstairs," he called to her, and she shut off the blow dryer just long enough to reply.

"Okay. I should be ready in about fifteen minutes."

"Got it," he said, glad that she wasn't the high-maintenance type. She always looked put together, but she also didn't spend hours in front of the mirror...unlike Jeremy's girlfriend Sloane. And all right, "hours" might have been a slight exaggeration. Still, Jake knew that Sloane's perfectly styled hair and makeup worthy of an Instagram influencer couldn't happen all that quickly, either. But Jeremy didn't seem to mind, and he supposed that was the important thing.

Downstairs, Jake's dog Taffy came trotting up to him as soon as he entered the kitchen, her lopsided ears perking, extravagant tail waggling in anticipation.

"Sorry, Taffers," he told her as he bent down to give her ears a scratch. "I'm just getting some water. You already had breakfast, and lunch is hours off."

She cocked her head at him, then pawed his pant leg.

"No," he said, trying to sound stern and probably failing miserably.

Well, they *were* going to be leaving her alone for a while. One dog treat probably wasn't a bad idea.

He went to the pantry and got out the little plastic box for treats that he and Addie had bought at the Container Store during one of their infrequent trips to Phoenix to do some shopping. Taffy got up on her hind legs, dancing around in joy as he extracted a treat from the box and handed it to her.

"And that's all," he admonished the dog.

From behind him came a chuckle. "You know you're going to give her at least two more before we leave," Addie observed wryly.

About all he could do was shrug. "Okay, busted. But only one more."

"Uh-huh."

Since Taffy had already pretty much inhaled the first dog treat, she was ready to take the second one from him as soon as he got it out of the treat box and bent down to hand it to her. When Jake straightened up, he saw Addie standing in the doorway to the kitchen, dark green puffer jacket already pulled over the gray sweater and jeans she wore.

"Ready?" he asked, quite unnecessarily.

"Yes," she replied. "I'll hang here while you get your coat."

Right. He nodded and hurried out to the entryway so he could get his own jacket from the coat closet there. When he returned to the kitchen, Addie was kneeling down and petting Taffy, although she stood up almost as soon as he reappeared.

"I wish I knew what this was about," she said, and Jake shrugged.

"Well, we'll find out soon enough. Maybe Joanna is your Wilcox Secret Santa, and she wants to give you your present."

"You have Secret Santas?" Addie asked, looking slightly alarmed. "No one told me."

He went over and gave her a quick hug. "No, I was just teasing you. We used to do gift exchanges, but it started to get kind of out of hand, so we stopped. Anyway, even if the Wilcoxes were still doing the whole Secret Santa thing, we'd be exchanging gifts at the Christmas potluck, not doing a one-off at someone's house."

"Oh, right," she said, her brow smoothing once again. However, she still seemed a little on edge. Jake could guess why; he knew she wasn't really looking forward to the potluck. A Wilcox tradition since the 1940s, the get-together was always held at the *primus's* house, and as many Wilcoxes as could fit generally crammed themselves into the place. Some years, the weather was bad enough that the cousins from farther-flung places like Winslow and Holbrook and Page couldn't come, and so the crowd ended up being a lot more manageable.

This year, however, the weather didn't seem like it would be much of an issue.

And although Addie had met a lot of her Wilcox relatives over the past six months, it had never been at anything formal, only get-togethers like Laurel's party the night before or chance meetings at the movies or while shopping or whatever. She'd come right out and told Connor she didn't want any fuss made over her even if Jackson Wilcox had been her father, and he'd gone along with her wishes, although Jake got the impression that a lot of people were secretly disappointed by her reticence, since they wanted to meet the late *primus's* daughter.

The potluck, on the other hand, was something she really couldn't avoid. There was no way Connor would cancel it, and she'd be expected to attend…which meant she'd be facing hordes of Wilcox relatives for the first time. While Jake wouldn't call Addie shy, neither did she like being the center of attention, and he knew she'd been steeling herself as Christmas Day rapidly approached.

She didn't say anything else, though, only zipped up her jacket and retrieved her purse from where she'd left it on the kitchen counter the night before. Jake bent and patted Taffy's head one last time, and then he and Addie went out the back door so they could make their way to the detached garage.

With the weather so clear and dry, there wasn't any frost to speak of, despite the chilly air that greeted them. They got into his Jeep Wrangler, and he backed it out of the garage and made his way down to Route 66 so he could head eastward to Joanna's house.

Addie didn't seem inclined to speak, only

looked out the window as the sights of downtown Flagstaff passed by the car window. Soon enough, however, they were past the historic district and moving through a more commercial area, with car-repair shops and strip malls and the occasional motel left over from the glory days of the highway they currently traversed. Maybe she was just tired; they'd both had a little too much to drink the night before and had gone to bed later than they'd planned. Jake had woken up with a headache of his own, although two cups of coffee and a nice, hot shower had done their work in banishing it for the time being.

Or maybe she was just worrying about what Joanna wanted.

"My mom texted me a little while ago," he commented, figuring he might as well attempt some sort of conversation. "She said she wanted to move Christmas Eve dinner to six instead of seven, if that's all right with us."

Addie glanced away from the window. A bit of a smile touched her lips, so it looked to him as if she was all right with the change in plans. "Sure," she said. "I mean, we don't have anything else going on that day, do we?"

"Not really. I know we were talking about going to the movies, but since we hadn't decided on a show time yet or anything, we can go to an earlier show if we have to." Actually, Jake had been happy to hear that his mother wanted to have dinner earlier than she'd planned, just because that would give him more time to make sure everything at the house was perfect for his proposal to Addie. A little shiver of unease went over him at the thought of asking her to marry him. True, he had no reason to believe she wouldn't say yes… but what if she didn't?

"Then moving up dinner sounds fine." A pause, and then she added, "And your mom really doesn't want us to bring anything?"

"Just ourselves and a bottle of wine," he replied. "My mother is very possessive of Christmas Eve dinner. She always wants to do everything herself. Well, except the dishes. She's only too happy to draft us kids for clean-up duty."

The faint smile Addie had been wearing shifted into an outright grin. "Thanks for the warning."

Not that he planned to have her—or Sloane—lift a finger. No, he and Jeremy would handle dish duty. It wasn't as though they hadn't been doing that very thing for years. And he wanted to ensure Addie's first Christmas with his family was just about as perfect as he could make it. He knew she was already having a hard time as the holiday approached and she was reminded on a daily basis that she wouldn't be able to share it with her own mother. While he couldn't do much to lessen that hurt, he at least wanted her to feel comfortable with her new family.

They passed the mall, its parking lot crammed with cars as people frantically shopped in these last few days before Christmas, and headed down the hill toward Joanna's house. Jake pulled onto the dirt road that led to her property, a road that seemed to have collected a few more ruts since the last time he'd come this way. Well, his Jeep could handle the ruts, and he supposed the dry weather did have its benefits. At least they weren't grinding through mud and snow.

A pause at the solar-powered gate that protected the place, and then they were bouncing along the last hundred yards or so to reach the house. Its steeply pitched roof and rustic log siding practically screamed for a coating of snow, but of course, the roof was bare. Icicle lights dangled from the eaves along the porch, although they clearly had been shut off for the day.

Jake parked the Wrangler in front of the house, and he and Addie got out. Almost as soon as they'd mounted the porch steps, the door opened, and Joanna looked out at them. For a change, her long, shiny black hair—the hair she'd inherited from her Navajo mother—lay loose on her shoulders instead of pulled back in a braid or a ponytail, and she wore a red sweater along with her jeans and cowboy boots, and appeared cheerful enough.

"Thanks for coming over," she said. "I hope you're hungry—I baked cookies."

Maybe at other times of the year, ten-thirty in the morning might have been a little early for cookies. But this was Christmas week, and Jake knew he wouldn't turn down the offer. Joanna's cookies—from the gooey chocolate chunk variety to her delectable snickerdoodles—were legendary.

Echoing his thoughts, Addie said with a smile, "There's always room for cookies."

That comment made Joanna grin, and she stepped out of the way so the two of them could enter the house. No Christmas tree, but a garland of evergreen boughs decorated with red velvet bows accented the wide oak mantel on the river-stone fireplace, and the air inside the house smelled of vanilla and cinnamon.

"I've got regular Christmas cookies and then snickerdoodles, because those are my favorite," Joanna said as she led them toward the dining room. Sure enough, two big platters of cookies waited there, one batch brightly decorated with red and green icing and glittery sugar crystals, the other much more subdued with its dusting of cinnamon and sugar. Still, Jake had had Joanna's snickerdoodles, so he knew just how good they were.

He reached for one at once, while Addie selected a Christmas cookie shaped like a bell, coated in buttercream frosting and tipped with red and green accents. She might not have been with the Wilcox clan for very long, but she already knew better than to turn down Joanna's cookies.

"Some water, too?" she offered. "I don't have any milk."

"Water's fine," Jake mumbled through a bite of snickerdoodle.

Joanna's mouth twitched, but she only headed into the kitchen while he and Addie munched happily on their cookies. By the time his cousin returned, they were done and brushing the crumbs off their hands.

"We can go sit down in the living room," she said. "Now that you've taken the edge off, so to speak."

He wasn't so sure about that. Another cookie —or two, or three—sounded like a great idea. But since there was plenty to go around and he didn't want to seem greedy, Jake nodded and followed Joanna into the living room, where she took a seat in the faded wing chair off to one side of the couch, and he and Addie sank down onto the sofa. A fire burned in the hearth, warm and welcome. He'd always liked Joanna's house, but it could be a little drafty.

"Well, then," Joanna said as she laced her

fingers across a jean-clad knee. "I suppose this seems a little strange, me having you come out here like this."

Addie sent a sideways glance at Jake, and he allowed his shoulders to lift ever so slightly. "I don't know," he hedged. "I mean, this is the season for visits, I suppose."

His cousin raised a dubious eyebrow. "Am I really in the habit of inviting people over for 'visits'?"

No, she wasn't. Joanna tended to keep to herself. Jake had always figured she acted that way because of being raised for half her childhood on the Navajo nation with her mother, rather than growing up in Flagstaff with the rest of her Wilcox cousins, but her solitary habits had never bothered him. That was Joanna being...Joanna.

"I guess not," he said.

Next to him, Addie sipped from her glass of water before asking, "So...why did you ask us to come over?"

The faintly amused look Joanna had been wearing abruptly disappeared. She pushed up the sleeves of her sweater and frowned. "This weather...." she began, then stopped, letting the words trail off as though she didn't quite know what to say next.

"What about it?" Jake asked. "I mean, it's been pretty dry, but this has happened before."

"No," Joanna said, still with that shadow of worry pulling at her brows. "Not like this."

"What do you mean, 'not like this'?" Addie said. "Jake told me that you've had other years where it barely snowed around the holidays."

Joanna's lips pressed together. "Well, that's true, but this time around, it still didn't feel right to me, so I called Julie."

"Julie Turnbull is a cousin of ours who works at the Bellemont office of the weather service," Jake explained, since of course, Addie would have no idea who Julie was.

"Right," Joanna said, then continued. "Anyway, I called her because I figured she'd have some sort of explanation for what was going on. I mean, the online weather reports talk about 'blocking high pressure' and things like that, but it didn't seem to me to be enough for this dry spell to be so extreme."

"And did she have a reason for it?" Addie asked. She looked interested, but not too troubled. While her talent involved controlling the weather, she hadn't bothered to study meteorology all that much beyond the basics. "I'm not a scientist," she'd joked once to Jake when he'd asked her why she hadn't wanted to go into that field, considering where her magical gifts lay.

"She brought up the high pressure thing again, but then she started really analyzing the patterns, running them against the computer models the weather service uses in most situations like this." Joanna reached up to tuck a lock of hair behind her ear. Usually, it was an innocuous sort of gesture, but Jake didn't miss the way her hand shook slightly as she did so. "Julie couldn't find a real reason for it. I mean yes, there's high pressure keeping the storms well to the north and west of us, but it's not a normal pattern for December, to say the least."

"Well, the weather has been weird all over," Jake said reasonably. "I mean, remember how we barely had a monsoon season last year?"

"Yes, but this isn't the same thing." She paused for a few seconds before saying, "I think someone's blocking our storms."

3

Addie

I STARED AT JOANNA, WONDERING IF I'D heard her correctly. "Wait—you mean like the government or something?"

A shake of her head. One shining black lock of hair slipped over her shoulder as she moved. "No. I mean a witch or warlock."

Even as my eyes widened, Jake said, "Oh, come on, Joanna—that's impossible. Addie's the strongest weather-worker any of us has ever seen, and even she isn't powerful enough to control the weather of a third of a continent."

And thank God for that. My own powers were problematic enough…or at least, they used to be. Once Joanna had shown me how to corral them into submission, they honestly hadn't given me any trouble.

All the same, I could see why Jake would be skeptical of his cousin's claim. If none of them had come across a weather-worker with my strength, then it seemed impossible to believe that a witch or warlock might exist who had the necessary gifts to control wind currents over such a vast area.

"I know it sounds crazy," she said. "But the patterns just aren't natural. Julie's data backs that up. The most plausible explanation is that someone in the Pacific Northwest is messing with the weather patterns."

That did not sound good at all. I glanced over at Jake, whose mouth had pressed into a hard, worried line. "Who's the clan up there?" he asked, and Joanna shrugged.

"I don't know, actually. That's something you'd need to ask your brother."

Right. Jake's brother Jeremy had built up a database of all the witch clans based in the United States and was constantly adding bits and pieces of information to it. He would know who lived in the area.

Of course, even if we had a name for the clan that might...*might*...be responsible, how much good would that do us? I was still learning about the witching world, but I knew the various clans tended to stay out of each other's business. We couldn't exactly go marching up there and demand that they stop, well, whatever it was that they were doing.

If they were even responsible.

"But what would be the point?" I asked. "I mean, what possible reason would they have for screwing with our weather? Especially since it doesn't just affect us, but the other Arizona clans and the clans in California and Nevada."

Jake rubbed a hand over the stubble on his chin. "I have no idea. Unless they're somehow chummy with the Walkers in South Dakota, and they egged them on or something."

That theory sounded like a bit of a stretch. No, there was definitely no love lost between the Wilcoxes and the Walkers, not after Jeremy had hacked the Walker *prima's* bank accounts to coerce her into letting Sloane, her recently discovered granddaughter, come back to Flagstaff with him. Even so, a thousand miles separated the Walker clan from whichever clan lived in Washington State. I somehow doubted they had much —if any—contact with each other.

It seemed that Joanna thought the same thing, because she said, "No, I don't think so. Haven't the Walkers been lying pretty low lately?"

"Yeah," Jake replied. "Jeremy's been keeping

tabs on them, because he still doesn't quite trust them not to come after Sloane. But they've got a new *prima* and seem to be behaving themselves. I think Jeremy put the fear of God in them."

"Or at least the fear of being broke," I quipped, and he grinned.

"Fate worse than death for a witch clan," he said. His posture had relaxed slightly, and the warm twinkle I loved so much had returned to his velvety brown eyes. Although the news Joanna had delivered was upsetting, it looked to me as though he'd started to come to terms with it.

Joanna, however, didn't seem all that amused. "Well, I hope we can get to the bottom of it." Her eyes met mine, darker than Jake's, nearly black in their frame of sooty lashes. "What do you think, Addie? Is this sort of thing possible?"

For a minute, I wondered why in the world she was asking me. After all, she was older and had far more experience controlling the weather than I did.

But I realized that, even though she had more experience, my own magical gift was much stronger than hers, elemental, powerful. She could guide clouds from place to place and coax them to bring some much-needed rain, while I had the ability to make lightning strike on my command. My gift allowed me to reach out and touch the air currents, to sense where a storm would go even before it had begun to move. It made sense that she would think I might have more insight into the current situation than she.

As strong as my gift was, though, I hadn't worked with it that much. I didn't know its outer limits...and I wasn't sure whether I really wanted to.

Unfortunately, I knew I might have to test my talent, might have to do my best to see if the strange magic I'd been born with was up to the task of discovering whether our current dry spell's origin truly was supernatural.

"I don't know," I said. "But I guess I'll have to try to find out."

We didn't stay long at Joanna's after that. Jake and I both knew the best thing to do would be to head over to Trident and get Jeremy's input on what we might be up against, since, other than their cousin Marie, who'd made the study of the country's witch clans her unofficial hobby, Jeremy knew more about the other U.S. witchy families than anyone else.

With Christmas only a couple of days away, Jake had told his brother that he could take some time off if he wanted. However, I had the impression he knew the offer would be ignored, that Jeremy would keep going in to babysit his algorithms because he didn't know what else to do with himself.

Sloane was a very patient woman. I didn't know whether I would have been able to put up with Jeremy's computer obsessions. Jake could get pretty focused if the situation warranted it, but he was also fine with taking time off for an afternoon hike or a shopping trip or just a break to hang out at home with the dog. Then again, Sloane had decided to go back to school as well and finish the degree she'd abandoned a few years earlier, and so she didn't have a lot of free time, either. Technically, we were schoolmates, since she'd also enrolled at Northern Pines, but since I was a senior and she was a sophomore, our paths didn't cross that much. Sometimes we'd get together for coffee—tea in her case—and hang out in between classes, although our schedules differed enough that we didn't have too many opportunities for socializing.

We parked in the driveway and headed inside Trident headquarters. There wasn't room for a Christmas tree in the converted Craftsman house, but someone—Laurel, I guessed—had tried to make things a bit festive by framing the windows and doorways in tinsel and putting some potted poinsettias on the mantel of the nonfunctional fireplace in the main room. We found Jeremy there, sitting in front of one of the Mac Pro computers and typing away so quickly, his fingers were almost a blur.

"Thought you were taking the week off," he said without bothering to look away from the screen.

"I am," Jake replied amiably, with the ease of long practice. He'd spent enough time putting up with his brother's foibles that the rudeness rolled right off his back.

"We needed to ask you something," I said. "About the witch clans in the Pacific Northwest."

Jeremy's fingers stilled on the keyboard, and he swiveled in his office chair to stare back at us. Thanks to having Sloane around, he appeared a bit more presentable than the first time I'd met him, when his hair looked as though he'd cut it with a blender. Clearly, she had little patience for an unkempt boyfriend.

"What about them?"

"We're worried that this dry spell we're having isn't natural. Joanna and Julie both think the blocking high pressure might be witch-related."

Jeremy remained silent for a moment, appearing to take in that information. Then his dark gaze flickered over to me. "What do you think?"

"I—I don't know for sure," I stammered, caught off guard. "But I think it's something we need to look into. So…what do you know about the clans in the area?"

"Not a lot," he said, turning back to the computer. He minimized the window he was working on and typed a few lines of code, bringing up what looked like some sort of database. "Um…there are two clans in Washington State. The bigger one is the Freemans—they're all over the western half of the state. The other clan is the Elliotts. They have about the same amount of territory when it comes to acreage, but there aren't nearly as many cities in their region, so there aren't as many of them."

I absorbed that information and looked over at Jake. Although I didn't know whether actual numbers counted in these sorts of calculations, it made sense to me that the bigger clan probably was a more likely suspect. He seemed to be thinking about the same thing, because he said, "Do you know much about the Freemans?"

"Nope." Jeremy reached for the bottle of water sitting on the computer table and took a large swallow from it. "As far as I know, the Wilcoxes have never had any dealings with them at all. This database basically started out as a list of witch clans I got from Marie, and I add to it when I get new information. But since none of us have ever crossed paths with the Freemans, there isn't much we know." A pause there as a wicked light entered his eyes. He gave his knuckles a good crack—I tried not to wince—and started typing. "I can find out, though."

"You can?" I asked, then wondered why I should be surprised. After all, Jeremy's ability to play with data was practically legendary.

"Sure. I even developed a few algorithms for this sort of thing after I had to dig into the Walkers' personal information. Just give me a few minutes."

After making that request, he started typing away. Since it seemed better to leave him alone to work, Jake and I both headed into the kitchen so we could get some water for ourselves. He got a couple of bottles out of the refrigerator, handed one to me, and took a seat at the round table that had been placed off to one side.

"You think he's going to find anything?" I asked after I'd sat down as well and removed the cap from my bottle of water.

"Oh, he'll find something," Jake said. "Whether it's anything we can use is a different story, but he'll definitely get some intel on the

Freemans. The amount of stuff he dug up on the Walkers was kind of amazing. For all I know, that could be another reason why they haven't wanted to make a stink about Sloane—Jeremy's got information on every real estate deal and business transaction they've been involved in since they came to the Dakota Territories in the 1870s."

Whatever Jeremy's faults, no one could ever accuse him of not being thorough. "Blackmail material?"

Jake grinned. "Possibly."

Since what I'd heard of the Walker clan was less than flattering, to say the least, I didn't bother to protest that blackmail was illegal. They'd brought their troubles on themselves.

Our own issues were a lot more immediate. I'd checked the weather app on my phone that morning before I got in the shower in the vain hope that maybe something might have changed in the seven-day forecast, but no such luck. It looked like highs in the upper thirties and lower forties with zero chance of precipitation for the foreseeable future. I should have known the universe wasn't going to give me that kind of help.

Then I wanted to scold myself. All right, the weather was a problem. But since the universe had also done me the kindness of sending Jake into my life, I really couldn't give it too much grief.

"Maybe I should try to see if I can use my talent to find out what's really happening," I suggested. "I mean, anything Jeremy finds might help, but on the other hand, even if we can pin down exactly who's behind this weird weather pattern, that doesn't mean we can get them to fix it."

Jake tapped his fingers against the side of the water bottle he held. Head tilted slightly, he asked, "Can you do that?"

"I have no idea," I said. "I haven't really done much to work with my gift after Joanna showed me how to control it."

"Well, except using targeted lightning strikes to knock out the SED's power plant," he responded, mouth curved in amusement.

"Okay, except that." I paused for a moment, recalling how I'd reached into the storm clouds over Alexandria to awaken the lightning and direct it to hit the same target over and over again. There hadn't been any joy in that destruction, only a terrible need to do whatever was necessary to free Jake and the rest of the witches and warlocks who'd been held in the government facility in Virginia. But at the same time, I hadn't really stretched my abilities in calling the lightning, had only intensified what I already knew how to do.

This...using my talent to find the magic

behind wind currents hundreds and hundreds of miles away…would be completely different.

"But sure, go ahead and try," Jake said then, his tone much gentler. Maybe he'd seen a shift in my expression and realized that I feared this particular situation would finally show me the limits of my magic.

I nodded and got up from my chair. "I think this'll work better if I'm outside," I told him. "You can stay here."

Although I'd made it sound as though remaining in the kitchen was his choice, I really meant that I needed him to stay inside so I could work without interruption. He seemed to understand what I was saying, because he said, "Sure," and took another swallow of water.

Since I'd only unzipped my jacket when I came inside rather than taking it off altogether, all I had to do was zip it back up and then let myself out the door and onto the back porch. The morning air had warmed a few degrees since Jake and I left our house, but it was still very chilly. I shoved my hands in my jacket pockets and descended the porch steps, spurred by the vague notion that since I'd come outside anyway, I needed to be all the way in the open rather than standing on the back porch.

In a way, taking up a position in the middle of the frost-yellowed grass felt better, because out there I was in full sunlight, letting it touch my hair and soak into the dark green jacket I wore. While the Trident Enterprises house had neighbors to either side, I doubted anyone at home would be standing out in the icy air and taking in the sun. At least, I had to hope they wouldn't.

Feeling vaguely foolish despite the lack of an audience, I closed my eyes and raised my arms. Maybe doing so wouldn't help at all, or maybe it would allow me to tighten my focus. I was new to all this, just feeling my way along.

Joanna had taught me how to allow my magic to reach out and sense the currents in the air, and that was what I did then. This time, however, I didn't stop a few miles away, but let that strange weather sense of mine travel with the wind—or rather, against the wind, since I needed to go where the wind had come from and not where it was heading.

So many miles that wind had traveled, all the way from the northern Pacific, where it took its strength from the frigid air that forever swirled above the North Pole. As I moved closer to its source, I began to sense a wrongness, something unnatural about the currents of the wind. The focus seemed to be somewhere over a large city— Seattle? Maybe, although I only got an impression of many buildings and people, and nothing specific.

Whatever the wrongness was, its effects rippled down to the south and east, shunting any moisture that would have come our way far to the west. I knew I'd read somewhere that California was having a very wet December, which I knew was good for them, considering the droughts that came and went in the state with frightening regularity.

But Arizona needed that moisture, too.

I opened my eyes, blinking a little against the bright winter sunshine. The wrongness I'd sensed still hovered in the back of my mind, plucking against my thoughts like an out-of-tune guitar string. Well, if nothing else, I'd learned that I didn't need to have my eyes closed in order to focus my ability.

A breath to center myself again, and I let my gift ride with the wind, following it back to the strange, dissonant note I'd detected. No—it wasn't one note, but several, as if more than one consciousness had summoned the wrongness.

Several witches or warlocks working together?

Maybe. I knew that Connor and Angela sometimes pooled their enormous gifts to make them even more powerful, like the time they'd teleported all the way to Virginia to rescue me from the SED facility in Alexandria, so such a thing wasn't completely unheard of. Still, I really didn't like the idea of there being another pair of witch-kind who might be equally strong. Connor's talents might have seemed unnerving, but he was my brother, and Angela my sister-in-law. I knew I could trust them.

But complete strangers—possibly Freeman witches—with the same kind of power?

That possibility opened up a whole new set of problems.

"Addie."

I turned. Jake stood on the back porch, Jeremy next to him. "You found something?" I asked.

"Maybe," Jeremy said. "Did you?"

"There's definitely something very weird out there," I replied. "And it feels as though it might be coming from several different people, not just one. But I couldn't get anything more than that."

The two brothers exchanged a glance. Jake looked troubled, but he sent a smile in my direction and said, "Well, come on inside so we can take a look at what Jeremy dug up."

No arguments from me. As soon as Jake said my name, my concentration had been broken, and I'd lost the thread I was trying to follow. Possibly, if I forced myself to focus again, I could get it back, but I'd try again later if I had to. For the moment, I realized how cold it really was outside, how I'd much rather be back inside the warmth of the house.

I mounted the steps to the back porch, then followed Jake and Jeremy into the converted dining room that was now the PC lab. Jeremy took a seat at one of the computers there, fingers flying as multiple documents started popping up on the paired screens in front of him.

Without looking back at me or Jake, he said, "I got a bunch of stuff—copies of deeds and trusts, bank records…the usual. All I was really trying to do was get a profile of people named Freeman in the area. There are a bunch of them, probably as many of them as there are Wilcoxes. I still haven't quite figured out who the *prima* is, although I think I've got it narrowed down to three people. Actually, though, I don't think the *prima* is the person we need to be concerned with. And after what you just said about having it feel as if several different people might be connected to our little problem, I'm even more convinced."

Jake shoved his hands in the pockets of his jeans. "So, what did you find?"

"I figured I might as well try to focus on anyone connected to the Freemans who seemed as if they might have some kind of weather powers."

I could feel my eyebrows lifting. "You can narrow your searches down that much?"

Jeremy must have wanted to see my dubious expression for himself, because he spun his office chair around so he faced me. However, he didn't appear annoyed. If anything, he seemed pleased that I'd questioned his findings.

"I've programmed in a bunch of parameters to work in concert with the algorithmic searches I used to locate possible Freeman witches and warlocks. Actually, it's a lot of the same data-crunching I do when I'm looking for our 'orphans.' And in this case, it found something extremely anomalous."

"Which was…?" Jake probed. Judging by the look on his face, he was used to his brother's somewhat long-winded explanations but still preferred that Jeremy cut to the chase.

"These two." He swiveled back in his chair so he faced the computer screens again, and typed in a few commands.

At once, the screens were filled with the faces of a pair of women, although they looked so alike, I had to glance back and forth between the two of them once or twice before I could reassure myself that they really were two different people. They looked like they might be around my age or maybe a little older, both of them with light brown hair that waved over their shoulders and big brown eyes. Pretty, with their oval faces and short, straight noses.

"Who are they?" I asked.

"Linda and Lori Freeman. Twins," Jeremy added, pointing out the obvious.

"What's so special about them?" Jake said. "I mean, besides being twins."

Which in itself wasn't so strange. It wasn't as though witches and warlocks didn't have twins; my nephew and niece, Ian and Emily, were twins.

"They have the same power," Jeremy replied, and Jake frowned.

His response made me ask, "Is that unusual?"

"Yes," Jake said. "Even in cases of identical twins, they don't generally have the same kind of magical talents. Actually, I don't know if I've ever heard of a case like that."

"I have," Jeremy told him. "I guess our great-great-whatever grandfather Edmund Wilcox's granddaughter had twin boys, and they had the same talent." As Jake's eyebrows began to lift in question, his brother went on, "I read about it in some old diaries Marie lent me to digitize. Anyway, even though it was kind of unusual, their gift was with growing things, so it wasn't as though it was something they could really abuse."

"Unless they made everything go wild and sent ivy climbing all over the place or something," I said, and Jeremy shot me a sour look.

"As far as I can tell, that didn't happen. Anyway," he continued, his tone quelling enough that I knew I'd better forbear from making any further quips, "this is all just speculation, but I think that Linda and Lori here both have your talent, Addie."

"Weather-workers?"

He nodded.

Jake didn't look completely convinced. After rubbing the scruff on his jaw and staring at the images of the twins for a few more seconds, he said, "How could you know that for sure?"

"Same way I found Addie," he replied calmly. It didn't seem as if he was too worried about his brother trying to poke holes in his story. "Weather anomalies. Of course, those seemed to end pretty quickly just a few weeks after their eleventh birthday, probably because someone in their clan walked them through how to control their talents. But the real kicker is that they both have master's degrees in meteorology."

That did seem to be a pretty convincing piece of evidence. All right, plenty of people studied meteorology who didn't have weather-working ability, but still, for both sisters to have pursued the same field of study and also to have strange weather phenomena associated with them seemed suspicious, to say the least.

As far as I could tell, Jake seemed to be thinking basically the same thing. Rather than argue further, he said, "Okay...so we have a pretty good idea as to who's behind our weather blockage. But why?"

"It's been drier than normal in the Pacific Northwest for the past three years," Jeremy replied. "Looks to me like they finally decided to do something about it. And it's working—for them, anyway. It's been raining all up and down the West Coast for almost a week now. Of course, the downside is that they're keeping all that moisture away from the rest of us."

Again, I couldn't argue with his theory. I'd felt the blockage in question with my weather sense, could tell there was nothing natural about it. Only....

"Even if you're right—" I began.

"I am," Jeremy cut in, tone so emphatic that I knew better than to argue with him.

I shrugged. "Okay, say you're right. What are we supposed to do about it?"

For the first time, Jeremy appeared less than confident. His hands remained resting on the keyboard, as if he wasn't quite sure what to do with them. "Um...tell Connor, I guess. He's the *primus*. He's the one who should reach out to the Freeman *prima* and tell her that what her weather-workers are doing is hurting a whole lot of people."

On the surface, I supposed that was the correct thing to do. I hadn't been a part of the Wilcox clan for very long, but I'd learned early on that there were channels involved when it came to reaching out to other witch families. Why those protocols had evolved, I had no idea. Still, it wasn't as though I could just pick up the phone and tell Lisa and Lori Freeman to lay off before they created another Dustbowl.

Or…could I?

"Do you have any contact info for them?" I asked suddenly. "Phone numbers…email addresses?"

"Of course," Jeremy replied. His tone seemed to indicate he was offended that I'd thought he wouldn't have dug up such basic information while conducting his investigation.

Apparently putting two and two together, Jake held up a warning hand. "Addie, I'm not sure that's such a good idea."

"Why not?" I said. "I don't know why we have to get all official and drag Connor into this. It's almost Christmas, and he's got three kids. He has other things to be worrying about."

Jake and Jeremy looked at each other. From the glint in Jeremy's eyes, I had a feeling he agreed with me. Jake, on the other hand, didn't appear convinced.

"Addie, he's the *primus*. He's supposed to get involved with matters regarding other clans."

I reminded myself that one of the things I loved about Jake was his sense of responsibility. No, he wasn't a hardcore by-the-book sort of person, but he also weighed his decisions carefully. I could tell he didn't want to be the instigator of another inter-clan incident.

"True," I said, speaking slowly as I built the argument in my thoughts before saying the words, "but we're basing all of this on conjecture. I honestly don't see what a harmless little email could do. I'd be the one to send it—one weather-worker reaching out to another. Wouldn't it be easier to handle it that way than turning into a big official thing? We don't know if the Freeman witches even have any idea about the side effects their weather experiment is causing."

A long pause. Jake rubbed his chin again, clearly torn. It seemed obvious to me that he also didn't want to bother Connor at such a busy time of year.

"All right," he said at last. "But let's talk about it first and figure out the best way to handle this. Okay?"

"Okay," I agreed.

"You rebel," Jeremy said with a grin. He typed something, and one of the laser-jet printers in the PC lab came to life.

I went over to it and waited as it spat out a couple of pieces of paper. When I pulled them out of the tray, I saw there was an info sheet for each twin, with phone numbers and addresses—both work and home—and various email addresses as well. Lisa worked for a Seattle news station, while Lori was employed at the local branch of the National Weather Service.

Holding them in one hand, I walked back over to Jeremy's workstation and gave the sheets of paper to Jake. "You can choose who to contact," I told him.

He didn't look quite as honored by the request as I'd thought. Carefully folding the papers in half and then half again, he said, "Let's take a break before we do that. It's almost lunch."

"Oh, crap, is it?" Jeremy interjected. He peered at the time stamp on the computer screens in front of him. "I'm supposed to meet Sloane for lunch. You two figure it out and then let me know what you decide to do."

"Okay," Jake said. He paused for a moment, and I wondered if he was going to try to invite us along to Jeremy's lunch with Sloane. However, he only said, "We need to get some lunch, too. I'll give you a call later."

Jeremy just nodded, since he was in the process of logging out of his computer. We took that as a signal to leave, and headed out to where Jake had left his Wrangler parked in front of the house.

"Are we really going to lunch?" I asked. Yes, we needed to eat, but I'd figured we'd go back to our place and scrounge.

"Yes," he said, and left it at that.

Since I could tell his thoughts were going a mile a minute, I stayed silent as we drove away from Trident Enterprises.

I could only hope he wasn't coming up with reasons to back out of the plan.

4

Jake

At least they'd been given a quiet booth in a corner at Murphy's Pub. That way, he didn't have to worry about anyone listening to their conversation.

And he needed a drink.

Once their waitress had set a Guinness in front of him and a glass of hard cider in front of Addie, Jake pulled out the pieces of paper she'd given him and set them down on the table, smoothing the creases from being folded up in his pocket.

Those printouts seemed innocuous enough— just a few lines on each sheet of paper with addresses, phone numbers, email addresses.

But he knew this whole thing could go sideways if they didn't tread carefully. Jeremy didn't seem to have dug up anything about the Freeman clan that appeared to prove they were as evil as the Walkers of South Dakota, but that didn't mean much. The sort of evildoing a witch clan could get up to wasn't necessarily the sort of thing that would show up on a financial statement.

"It's going to be okay," Addie said, offering him an encouraging smile before she picked up her pint of cider and took a sip.

"Probably," he allowed. "But still…."

She was quiet for a few seconds, appearing to gather her thoughts. "Well, what's the worst that could happen?"

The question wasn't a throwaway line; it seemed obvious to him that she genuinely wanted to know. Growing up outside a witch clan put a person at a definite disadvantage when it came to sussing out the finer details of inter-clan etiquette.

"'The worst'?" he repeated, and pushed a hand through his hair before picking up his glass of stout. "The *prima* of the Freemans finds out that we've been in touch with members of her clan without asking for permission, and she makes a stink about it."

"But what can she actually *do?*" Addie persisted. "I mean, Seattle is a long way from Flagstaff. If they were right next door, it would be one thing, but…."

Well, that was the crux of the matter. Maybe the Freeman *prima* couldn't do much at all. Or maybe she had some kind of scary power like the former *prima* of the Walkers, the power to control people with her mind or something even worse, and she'd figure out a way to retaliate. Jake knew he didn't want to be responsible for bringing that kind of trouble to the Wilcox clan…and he somehow doubted Addie did, either. If Connor was the person reaching out, that would be one thing, but….

He stopped there and stared across the table at her. She blinked, beautiful gray-green eyes full of puzzlement.

"What is it?"

"You're the *primus's* sister."

"Well, yeah," she responded, as if such a fact should be patently obvious.

Jake shook his head. "No, what I mean is, the situation is a little different if it's the sister of the *primus* who's making the contact. If it was coming from me, it would be one thing—I'm nobody —but—"

"You are not 'nobody,'" she cut in, her tone a gentle rebuke.

"Thanks for the vote of confidence," he said with a grin. "All I'm saying is that I'm just a random Wilcox. But witch clans are all about tradition, and it's traditional that the immediate family of the *prima* or *primus* has a little bit more clout than the rest of us."

"Then I'll call," Addie said. She reached over and pulled the papers toward her, arched brows drawing together slightly as she looked down at the information they contained. "Or maybe an email would be better. It's less intrusive."

Possibly, but an email also left a paper trail. A phone call would be safer. "I'd call if I were you."

She pursed her lips but didn't reply. Jake knew she didn't like the phone, preferred to text or email if necessary, and yet he guessed she wouldn't argue this particular point with him.

"All right," she said after a long pause. "Who do you think I should call?"

"Which one works at the National Weather Service?"

A brief glance at the papers down on the table, and Addie replied, "Lori."

"Then I'd call her. I have a feeling her hours might be a little less crazy than her sister's schedule at the TV station." Or at least, Jake hoped that would be the case. Maybe Lori had the overnight shift. He had a vague idea that someone had to be on duty all the time at a place like that, since of course the weather didn't exactly follow a nine-to-five schedule. Well, they'd give it a try, and if Lori wasn't available, they'd reach out to her twin sister.

Looking resigned, Addie said, "All right. I guess I'll call when we get back to the house."

Since Jeremy had provided both work and home numbers, Jake figured that should be all right, even though it was only the early afternoon. Worst case, Addie could leave a message at the home number—which might be Lori Freeman's cell phone. It was hard to know these days, with fewer and fewer people having landlines.

But since that matter seemed to have been handled for the time being, Jake figured it was better to let the matter go. He asked an innocuous question about Addie's class schedule for the spring semester, and she accepted the obvious change of subject with relief. They had a quiet lunch after that, and went home to find their dog Taffy utterly disgusted with them for having the temerity to go out to eat rather than having lunch at home so she could beg scraps from them.

He ruffled the dog's ears and gave her an extra treat after she was done with her kibble, Addie looking on the whole time with an indulgent smile on her lips. Luckily for him, she was totally on board with spoiling their pet, too, so he didn't have to worry about her giving him any crap for feeding the dog too many treats. If Taffy had been a pudgy dog, maybe those treats would have been a problem, but she was just as wiry and as full of energy now as the day he'd found her five years ago.

Addie took her cell phone and the piece of paper with Lori Freeman's information on it into the family room, then sat down on the sofa there. With Taffy still dancing around his legs, hoping for another treat, Jake followed her and seated himself as well. Should he reach over and give her fingers an encouraging squeeze?

No, probably not; she had the phone in one hand and the piece of paper in the other. Since she'd steeled herself to do this, he had a feeling it wouldn't be a good idea to distract her.

One hand absently petting his dog's head, he waited while Addie entered the woman's number in her phone and touched her finger to the green button on the screen to connect the call. A moment passed, and Addie straightened.

"Hi," she said, in a bright, too cheery sort of voice that didn't sound much like her. "My name is Addie Grant, and I'm calling about a weather-related question. If you could give me a call back at your convenience, I'd really appreciate it. My number is 928-555-8766. Thanks!"

As soon as she was done speaking, she pulled the phone away from her ear and set it down on the coffee table, her expression both rueful and annoyed.

"Voicemail," she explained, although Jake had

already guessed that she wasn't speaking to a live person.

"Well, you tried," he said. "And Seattle is an hour behind us at this time of year, so she might've been on a lunch break or something. There's plenty of time for her to call you back."

Immediately, she appeared relieved. "Oh, right. I'd forgotten about that. Well, I guess we just have to hang and see what happens."

"And if she doesn't return your call, we'll try Lisa," Jake responded. "Although I like how you said it was a 'weather-related question.' It's not even a lie, but it also sounds totally innocuous."

"Here's hoping." Addie moved closer to him, snuggling up against his body so she could lay her head on his shoulder. "What should we do while we're waiting?"

He felt the heat of her body even through the sweatshirt he was wearing and thought of a few things he'd like to do. Problem was, he doubted it would be a good idea to push her down onto the sofa cushions and make love to her when she might get a call back at any minute, and so he told himself he'd have to take a rain check on that one.

Hopefully, not for too long. His need for her hadn't lessened during the six months they'd been together, and he couldn't stop himself from thinking about the moment when he asked her to be his wife. With all that was going on, maybe he should wait until New Year's Eve to pop the question.

No, that didn't feel right. Whatever happened, he didn't want to wait much longer to make sure she would always be at his side.

Addie

We settled in to watch a marathon of *Nailed It* on Netflix, mostly because it was the sort of thing we could easily pause if and when Lori Freeman returned my call, and also because watching a baking show seemed like the sort of thing you should do with only a few days until Christmas. The time ticked past, and I found my gaze continuing to flicker toward the clock on the mantel across the room. After we watched three episodes, Jake got up to start a fire in the gas fireplace, and the room felt cozy and deliciously warm.

Or at least, it would have been cozy if I hadn't been so on edge. We hadn't really settled on a cut-off time for when we'd give up on Lori and try to contact her twin sister Lisa, but it was getting close to five o'clock and we still hadn't heard a damn thing.

It's only four in Seattle, I reminded myself,

but the thought still wasn't terribly reassuring. Maybe Lori Freeman's work kept her so busy that she didn't even have five minutes to spare to return a phone call, and yet I couldn't quite keep myself from wondering if she'd somehow sensed I was a witch and that was the reason why she hadn't been in contact.

Which I knew was ridiculous. Yes, witches and warlocks could sense the presence of another of their kind, but only when they were within a yard or so of each other. It wasn't as though Lori Freeman would listen to my message and instantly deduce that I was a fellow witch. If I'd called myself "Addie Wilcox," then sure, that last name would have set off alarm bells, but "Addie Grant" shouldn't mean anything to her. Maybe I shouldn't have been quite so vague in my message. It did sound sort of like the kind of thing a person might easily ignore.

And so on. My brain kept chattering away in the background as I kept only half my focus on the TV. Jake could probably tell that I was distracted, but he didn't try to probe, only sat next to me on the couch and offered to refill my water glass from time to time. We'd put the ingredients for a simple pot roast and vegetables in the crock pot before we'd even left for Joanna's that morning, so it wasn't as if we had to worry too much about getting dinner together when the time came, beyond throwing together a salad and pouring some wine.

At a couple of minutes after six, my cell phone started to ring. I sat bolt upright and grabbed for it where it sat on the coffee table, while Jake seized the remote and paused the show we were watching.

"Addie Grant?"

A woman's voice, unfamiliar, although she sounded halfway puzzled, as if she was trying to figure out if we had some kind of past connection that she'd somehow overlooked.

"Yes, I'm Addie," I said. "Is this Lori Freeman?"

"Yes." A pause, and she went on, "You had a weather question?"

Here we go. I pulled in a breath, reminded myself that fortune favored the bold, and said, "It's about the massive ridge of high pressure that's keeping all the precipitation trapped on the West Coast."

For one long, painful moment, she didn't say anything. When she spoke, her tone was neutral...far too neutral. "It's a little unusual," she replied. "But these sorts of weather patterns do set up from time to time."

A careful answer, one I knew she was hoping would be enough to put me off. But she wouldn't be able to evade making a useful response to my next comment quite so easily. "I suppose so," I said. "Except you and I both know that this one isn't exactly natural."

"I don't know what you're talking about," she responded, her tone flat.

"I think you do," I told her, even as I prayed inwardly that I wasn't making a huge fool out of myself. What if it turned out that Lori and Lisa Freeman didn't have anything to do with the strange weather after all? But since I'd committed myself to this particular confrontation, I had to press on. "I know there's nothing natural about this particular weather pattern because I can work with weather the same way you can."

"Oh, you work for the Weather Service?"

Nice try. "Not exactly," I said. "I'm a weatherworker, a witch. Just like you and your sister are."

Dead silence. I risked a glance over at Jake and saw that he'd shifted so he was perched on the edge of the sofa cushion, intently listening to my every word. Belatedly, I realized that maybe I should have put the call on speaker, but I'd been nervous enough that the thought hadn't really crossed my mind. Anyway, I always thought it was sort of rude to do such a thing without asking for permission first.

Lori Freeman gave a fake-sounding laugh and said, "Look, I don't know what kind of joke you're trying to pull on me, but I don't think it's very funny. I'm going to hang up."

"Don't," I said desperately. "Look, I'm with the Wilcox clan in Flagstaff. My brother is the *primus* here. I can tell something very weird is going on with the weather, and it seems to be centered in Seattle. And whatever's going on, it's affecting us here in Arizona and in other parts of the Southwest."

Once again, all I heard from the phone was silence. I glanced down at the screen to confirm the call was still connected, which it was. Lori was definitely on the other end of the line, even if she didn't seem inclined to reply to my comments.

At last, though, the sound of an expelled breath emerged from the phone's speaker and she said, "We didn't mean for this to happen."

Those words made a flare of triumph go through me. Maybe it wasn't an outright admission, but her response was still good enough for my purposes. "You and your sister?"

"Yes. We—well, we'd been suffering a pretty bad drought for the past several years. Lisa and I finally decided to try to do something about it. We thought that maybe if we worked together... pooled our powers, so to speak...then maybe we could break down the weather systems that had been shunting storms to the north and south of us."

"And it worked." I didn't phrase the words as a question, mostly because it was fairly obvious to anyone who'd been paying attention that Seattle definitely wasn't dealing with a drought any longer.

"It worked," she replied, her tone heavy. "It worked too well. I noticed fairly soon afterward that our spell was keeping all the moisture concentrated on the West Coast. So, I told Lisa, and we decided to reverse what we'd done."

"But?" I asked. Obviously, that reversal hadn't worked so well, or we wouldn't have been having our current conversation.

"But nothing happened. We've been trying ever since then to undo what we've done, and nothing is working." Voice tight with desperation, she went on, "You have to believe me. We wouldn't have done something like this if we'd had any indication that it was going to go so horribly wrong."

She sounded so upset that I knew she had to be telling me the truth. Inwardly, I couldn't help being relieved. Okay, the current situation was far from optimal, but at least I knew it was the result of an honest mistake and not due to some sort of malign intent.

"Oh, I believe you," I said quickly. While I hadn't really planned on having to make reassurances during our phone call, I knew I had to make sure she understood that the Wilcoxes had no plans to retaliate against the Freemans. No, we just wanted to get things back on track as quickly as possible. "But...maybe if you had someone in your clan help you? Maybe your *prima?*"

"No, that wouldn't work," Lori replied. "Her talent isn't anything that could help with this. Besides, she'd blow a gasket if she found out what Lisa and I have done. And my sister and I are the clan's only weather-workers right now. There isn't anyone who could step in."

Well, crap. I had a feeling this wouldn't be easy, or the two sisters would have fixed the situation already. Still, I really didn't want to believe there wasn't anything anyone could do.

She went on, now sounding almost painfully eager, "But...you said you're a weather-worker. You must be a strong one, or you wouldn't have been able to detect something wrong about the current weather pattern from so far away."

"Um...maybe," I hedged. I really didn't like to think about how my particular ability was stronger than that of anyone else with the weather-working gift. It made me feel as though people looked at me like some sort of chosen one or whatever, which couldn't be further from the truth. My talent might have helped me out of a few tight spots, but it certainly wasn't going to help me save the world or anything.

But apparently my hesitant agreement was enough for Lori to latch on to, because she said, "If you're that strong, then maybe you can do something to fix this."

"I don't know—" I began.

"You might, though," she cut in. "Why not try? Lisa and I have been banging our heads against this for more than a week now and haven't had any luck. What could it hurt to see if your magic might work where ours failed?"

"Because I might make things even worse," I said.

"Or you could fix them," she said. "And then we could put this thing behind us."

While you keep the mess away from your prima, I thought, although I didn't say anything. Honestly, if our situations had been reversed, I probably would have been doing my best to keep the whole thing from my clan leader, too. Or maybe not. I had a feeling Connor would at least try to be understanding, while I had no idea what the Freeman *prima* was like. Maybe she was a real hard-ass.

However, I realized we didn't have a whole lot of options. The current situation couldn't go on indefinitely, and it sounded as though whatever spell Lora and Lisa had conjured up between them, it was a doozy. Honestly, the whole idea of a spell sounded strange to me, since I certainly didn't have to cast any spells to make my weather magic work, and it wasn't as if Jake had to utter a sequence of words to move objects with his mind, or Jeremy had to draw some kind of magical diagram to summon his crazy ability to make computers do whatever he wanted them to.

But maybe other clans did things differently, or maybe the spell had been a way for the twins to bind their individual powers together and make them stronger. I knew I was wandering into the unknown here, and about all I could do was see if I could make any kind of difference at all.

"Did you write down your spell?" I asked. "It might help if I could take a look at it."

"We did," Lori replied. The relief in her voice was obvious, probably because my question had signaled that I would at least try to make a stab at things and see if I could fix the problem they'd created. "I can email it to you."

"Sure, do that," I said. "My email address is agrant928@gmail.com."

A pause, during which she was probably writing down the information. "Got it. I'm just wrapping up things at the office, but I'll send it to you as soon as I get home."

"Great," I replied, although inwardly, I wasn't feeling quite as upbeat. So, she was sending me the spell. Would I be able to do a damn thing with it?

Well, I wouldn't know until I took a look at the thing. And maybe Jake or Connor would have some words of advice for me. They had to have a little more experience at this sort of magic, even if the Wilcox clan wasn't really into using spells to focus their abilities.

"Then I'll let you go," I said next, since it seemed obvious that I couldn't do much else. I had to wait for Lori to send me the spell before I could even start to plan my next step. "Thanks for returning my call."

"No, thank you," she said. "I hope—I hope we can fix this. I'll be home in about a half hour, so keep an eye out for my email sometime after that."

"I will," I promised. "Drive safe."

We ended the call there, and I put the phone back down on the coffee table and met Jake's eyes. He was frowning slightly—not because he was worried or upset with me, but more because he was trying to process the side of the conversation he'd overheard.

"So, they really did do it," he said.

"Looks that way. And she thinks I can just swoop in and make everything better."

His hand stole into mine and gave it a reassuring squeeze. "You have an amazing talent, Addie. If anyone can fix this, it's you."

Although I appreciated his confidence in me, I

didn't think I could allow myself to be quite so hopeful. After all, I was stepping into brand-new territory with this particular problem. "Maybe with Joanna's help," I said dubiously, and he nodded.

"That's actually a really good idea," he told me. "We have enough roast to feed three people, don't we?"

"At least three," I replied. "It's a big roast—we're probably going to be eating leftovers for days."

"Perfect. I'll text her and see if she can come over. That way, you can look at Lori's spell whenever it shows up."

I had to admit that having Joanna's assistance was infinitely preferable to going it alone with this thing. As Jake got out his phone, I sent him what I hoped was an encouraging smile.

At the same time, though, I wondered if Joanna would even be able to help. It was two witches working together who'd created the original mess, after all.

I didn't say anything, however. No, I only watched as he sent the text and hoped I hadn't just bitten off way more than I could chew.

5

Jake

JOANNA HAD BROUGHT A BOTTLE OF CABERNET with her, obviously trying to make this look at least a little like a social call. But as soon as she gave the bottle to Jake as they stood by the dining room table, she said crisply, "Let me see this spell you told me about."

Addie handed over the email she'd printed off from her laptop. "I don't know the first thing about spells," she confessed. "I didn't even realize that was really a thing with witches."

"It can be," Joanna replied, dark eyes scanning the few brief lines on the piece of printer paper. "It depends on the clan, and the witch or warlock in question. Some people find using spells helps their focus, or allows them to use their gifts in new ways. I've heard the de la Paz clan has a pretty big collection of spell books, but I don't know anything more than that."

While she was speaking, Jake had gone ahead and uncorked the bottle of cab and poured some into each of the glasses set out on the dining room table. He handed one to Joanna and one to Addie, and they both accepted them gratefully and took a sip.

"This looks pretty straightforward," Joanna went on, giving another glance down at the printed spell. "They're calling the rain and the storms, and invoking their twinned powers to give them the strength to make the spell effective."

"Well, that part definitely worked," Jake observed wryly.

"A little too well," Addie said. She frowned. "But if it was their twin powers that made this spell work in the first place, how are you and I supposed to undo it?"

"By working together as well." Joanna didn't look nearly as worried as Addie, but then, his cousin always appeared serene and untroubled by whatever messes might be taking place around her, whether that was managing fifty head of alpacas or sliding under her truck to drain the transmission fluid. "That seems to be the best thing to try. It could be that the Freeman twins' powers are too bound together, and so when they tried to undo the spell, they couldn't separate their own magic enough to get the reversal to work."

Jake thought that sounded like a plausible enough theory. He didn't know anything about twin powers—Connor and Angela's kids were too young for their magic to have begun to develop yet—but he could see how it might be hard to separate something that had always been basically inseparable.

"Tonight?" Addie asked, and Joanna shook her head.

"No, I'll need some time to study it, sleep on it. Can I keep this?" she asked, holding up the piece of paper with the spell.

At once, Addie nodded. "Sure. I'll just print myself another one."

"Good idea. You'll want to have it memorized before we try anything. If you're always looking down at a piece of paper while trying to say the words of a spell, you'll distract yourself, and loss of focus is never a good thing when dealing with magic like this."

Jake couldn't argue with that. "Well, the food's ready," he said, "so we should go ahead and eat."

No one had any apparent objections to that plan. Jake excused himself to go to the kitchen and bring in the platter with the roast and the bowl with the salad, then hurried back to get the vegetables and bread. Addie had looked as though she was going to protest, to offer to help him, but he'd given her a small shake of the head, hoping she'd figure out that he wanted her to stay at the table with Joanna.

Which she did, seating herself at the place to the right of the head of the table, while his cousin took the left. Addie filled everyone's glasses, and asked Joanna if she had any big plans for Christmas.

"Not really," she said. "I mean, beyond the potluck at Connor's place. My mother's still out in Kayenta, and she didn't want to make the trip to Flagstaff this year."

"Oh," Addie replied, sounding confused.

Jake set down the vegetables and the bread, then gave his cousin a quick, inquiring glance, wondering if it was okay to elaborate. He hadn't gone into a lot of detail with Addie about his cousin Joanna's past, partly because he didn't think it was his business to mention it in the first place, and partly because the subject had never really come up.

"My parents split up when I was ten," Joanna said, appearing to take pity on him. "That was when my powers started to appear. They were both worried about what Jackson might do if he learned the clan finally had a weather-worker, and so she took me with her back to the reservation while my father stayed in Flagstaff. About five years after that, my father remarried—a civilian woman. They have their own family, and I've just kind of…stayed out of it."

Addie absorbed all this information in silence, expression troubled. It seemed obvious enough to Jake she didn't much like the implication that her late father had been so power hungry, he wouldn't have scrupled to use a young weather-worker's talents to further his own ends. Well, no one had tried to whitewash the man Jackson Wilcox had been, but neither had his daughter been exposed to some of his more dubious schemes.

"Anyway," Joanna went on, "I've had my mother come stay with me at Christmas ever since I bought my house, but her eyesight isn't so great anymore, and she doesn't want to make the drive this year. Her place is small, so there isn't anywhere for me to stay if I go visit her. That's why I'm planning to stay here and kind of just do the Wilcox family thing."

"Then I'm extra glad you came to dinner tonight," Addie said, her tone almost fierce, as if she wanted to make sure Joanna knew she'd always have someplace to come hang out if she wished…especially around the holidays, when being alone could be tough. "Sort of a pre-Christmas get-together."

"I'm glad you invited me." Joanna glanced over at Jake. "Just like I'm sure my cousin here is glad about that plate of chocolate chunk cookies I brought over."

Truth be told, he was very glad about those cookies—when he and Addie had planned this meal, they'd thought it would just be the two of them, and so they hadn't gotten anything for dessert—but he only smiled back at Joanna and said, "Your company was all we needed."

A wicked light danced in her dark eyes, but she didn't bother to contradict him. "It is the season for family, after all."

They turned their attention to the food after that, and when the conversation picked up again, it was on neutral topics—whether there was going to be a big Wilcox contingent this year at the traditional midnight pinecone drop in downtown Flagstaff on New Year's Eve, or whether they should stay in and have a party at the house he and Addie shared. Privately, Jake would rather have a party; while they could walk to the New Year's celebrations and so didn't have to worry about drunk drivers or anything like that, it could be damn cold standing out there on San Francisco Street at nearly midnight. Better to stay home where it was warm and safe.

But this would be Addie's first New Year's in Flagstaff, and if she wanted to go to the pinecone drop, then of course he'd take her.

However, as the discussion flowed on, it

seemed pretty obvious to him that she'd rather stay home and play hostess. The house was really perfect for big parties, and although they'd had a couple of small get-togethers during the past few months, with Addie so busy at school, they really didn't have the time to do anything too elaborate. Planning would be easy enough—he knew Laurel would be more than happy to lend her assistance—and all they'd have to do was put out the call on the Wilcox grapevine to make sure everyone who might be interested knew about the event. True, they ran the risk of having too many people show up, but the Wilcoxes were generally good about that sort of thing. No one under twenty-one, and the older, more settled people with kids wouldn't show up at a New Year's blow-out hosted by a couple of twenty-somethings. It would be fine.

They made plans to have Joanna return the next morning around eleven so she and Addie could work on the counter-spell, and his cousin thanked them for dinner before driving off in her older but meticulously maintained Chevy Silverado truck.

"Well, that went okay," Addie observed as she began gathering up the dinner plates, although she didn't look particularly cheerful.

Jake hurried over to collect the serving plates, even as he guessed at the reason behind her somewhat downhearted expression. "Joanna's right—it's better to give yourself time to prepare for something like this. One more night without snow isn't going to hurt anything."

"I suppose so. Only...." The words trailed off, and she shook her head before taking her pile of plates into the kitchen so she could stack them on the counter next to the sink.

He followed her with his own collection of dirty dishes. "Only what?"

"Oh, nothing." She started the water running and opened the dishwasher. "I guess I was just hoping we could get this taken care of as quickly as possible. We've only got two more days until Christmas. What if we can't fix the weather before then?"

After putting the serving bowls and plates on the counter next to the rest of the dishes, he took a step back and crossed his arms. Part of him wanted to tell Addie that he could do the clean-up, but living with her for the past six months had taught him that she liked to lose herself in mindless chores when she was troubled about something. Better to let her do her thing.

"It's not the end of the world if we don't have a white Christmas," he said then, giving her the same piece of advice he'd handed to himself in the recent past. "We'll all be together, and that's the important thing."

"I know." A very small lift of her shoulders,

and she went on, "And I'm trying not to put too much pressure on myself. But this still isn't the sort of thing we can let continue forever, even if it doesn't snow on Christmas."

"And we won't let it go on forever." He came over and pressed a light kiss against her temple, one that let her know he was there and that he cared, but wouldn't interrupt her flow while she worked. "I just don't want you to stress too much. One way or another, we'll fix this."

She smiled then, her expression brightening. "I think that's what I love most about you. You can always make me feel better about stuff."

"Just doing my job, ma'am."

A grin crinkled her eyes, and she set a plate in the dishwasher before going on her tiptoes so she could kiss him full on the lips.

Yes, much better. Desire stirred in him, warm and welcome, and he wanted to pull her against him, soapy wet hands and all. The dishwasher was fairly new, but it was still temperamental enough that they needed to rinse everything pretty thoroughly before they dared to put anything in it.

Jake held off from hugging Addie, however, since she was almost finished. And when she was done, she dried her hands on a dishtowel and came over to him and put her arms around his waist. They kissed again, slowly, thoroughly, their lips tasting of chocolate and wine.

No words needed to be spoken. They walked up the stairs together, hand in hand, and went to the bedroom, where they reached for each other as they fell onto the bed, showing once again that all they really needed was the two of them together in the dark, making the world's ills go away.

If only for a short time.

Addie

We were both up early the next morning. Although I usually slept like a rock after one of Jake's and my lovemaking sessions, I tossed and turned, troubled by dreams of lightning and storms, images of creeks running wild with water that dried up as soon as I bent to trail my fingers through it.

I knew it was only my subconscious mind playing with me, but still, those mental pictures were unnerving. No, I wasn't a seer, didn't have the ability to look into the future and know what was going to happen next, and yet I would have much preferred not to dream at all...or at least, not have been able to recall those dreams when I awoke.

As best I could, I pushed the memory of my dreams away when I went in to take a shower.

Jake didn't seem to notice anything wrong, only told me he'd shower after he had some coffee, and that he'd make a big pot so there'd be plenty left over for me. It was basically the same thing he did every day, but I still appreciated the gesture.

Because we'd woken up so early, we were all too ready by the time Joanna showed up at ten. She didn't look too worried about the task that lay ahead of us, but maybe she was just good at hiding her emotions. I didn't really know, because we hadn't spent much time together in the months that I'd been living in Flagstaff. I was busy with school, and she had her alpacas to look after, and although she was the clan's other weather-worker, it wasn't as though we had all that much in common.

Still, I was grateful for her presence that morning. My gift was still fairly new to me, while she'd been working with hers for almost twenty years. The situation we faced might have been a novel one, but at least Joanna knew how to manage her magical talent.

She declined Jake's offer of some coffee and glanced over at me. "Ready?"

Well, I had to admit that she wasn't the sort of person to beat around the bush. Whether I actually was ready or not might have been a subject for some conjecture, but I also didn't see any point in delaying.

"I think so," I said. "I've got the spell memorized, so I don't think there's much other preparation I can do."

"No, all we can do now is try." A pause as she tilted her head to one side, considering. "I think we'd better go out in the backyard. It's easier to feel what the wind and the weather are doing outside, and it's private enough."

Which was true. Old, established trees sheltered the yard at our house, and even though half of them had long since shed their leaves, there were enough pines and fir that no one should be able to see what Joanna and I were doing. Not that I really expected any of our neighbors to be hanging out in their backyards on that frosty morning. No, I guessed they were either safely indoors or maybe out doing some last-minute Christmas shopping.

"Sounds good," I said.

Jake shifted his weight as he looked from me over to his cousin. "Is it okay if I go out with you, or would that be distracting?"

"No, you can come along," Joanna replied. "Although it's probably a good idea if you stay on the porch."

She didn't say, *And out of the way,* but I got that impression from her words. Apparently, Jake did, too, because he didn't argue, only nodded and said, "Sure."

Joanna hadn't taken off her coat, so she waited while Jake and I went to the hall closet and got out our jackets. Once we were zipped up and I'd wrapped a scarf around my throat for extra measure, we all headed outside. As requested, Jake took a seat in one of the Adirondack chairs on the back porch, while Joanna and I headed down the steps and made our way to the center of the lawn, now yellow and sad-looking. If this had been a normal winter, that dead grass would have been covered by a concealing blanket of snow, but right then, it seemed almost reproachful, as if it was trying to tell me that I'd somehow wounded it by letting the weather be so dry.

Logically, I knew that was ridiculous. The weather certainly wasn't my fault.

And, with any luck, Joanna and I would be able to fix things so the world could go back to normal, and we'd get the white Christmas we were all hoping for.

She paused a pace or two away from me, face tilted up toward the sky so her sleek black hair fell down her back like a waterfall. That morning, no clouds were in evidence, only a bright, hard blue that seemed to stretch on forever.

"Can you feel it?" she said in a low tone, barely more than a murmur.

I didn't have to ask what she was talking about. Already that morning, I'd reached out with my talent to feel the wrongness so many hundreds of miles away. In the back of my mind, I'd been hoping that the problem might have fixed itself, that I'd wake up that morning and discover the magical blockage had melted away overnight… but of course, we couldn't be that lucky.

"Yes," I replied. "It's still there. It hasn't moved or changed."

"In a way, that's good," she said, still in that soft, calm voice. "At least it hasn't gotten any bigger."

Honestly, that possibility hadn't even entered my mind. So yes, I needed to be grateful the situation hadn't worsened overnight. "What now?"

"We reverse the spell," Joanna said. "Think of the words. Hold them in your mind like a set of instructions. Then think of the best way to reverse the steps."

Looking at the problem that way made me a bit less nervous. "Instructions" sounded infinitely less dangerous than "spell." But in a way, that's exactly what Lisa and Lori Freeman's spell had been—a set of instructions to the universe telling it how to ease the drought that had plagued their region.

Now Joanna and I had to tell the universe that it had done its work and could let go.

I had to hope it would be listening.

Two of heart, together again

Banish sun and bring the rain.

Almost unconsciously, Joanna and I reached out to each other so we could join hands. Yes, that was right—our powers needed to be bound together just as Lisa and Lori's powers had combined to create such a powerful enchantment. We weren't twins or even sisters, but Wilcox blood flowed in our veins, and I had to hope that would be enough.

I imagined the high pressure that blocked the winter storms from coming our way like a high brick wall. We needed to pull it down brick by brick in order to allow the air currents to go their own way.

Was that a crack I sensed? It was almost like tugging a few stones from a dike and watching as a rivulet began to trickle its way outward from each opening. Small, yes, but if we kept pulling—

Joanna raised a hand to her forehead and staggered backward a pace, her hands slipping from mine. Almost at once, those small breaks in the spell that had been beginning to form disappeared as if they'd never been there at all. No...not when we were so close....

To my horror, she slumped to the ground, falling so her long, dark hair spread across the dead grass like a cloak. I reached for her, even as a screech of wood on the porch told me Jake had bolted from his chair so he could hurry down the porch stairs toward us.

"What happened?" he asked, then knelt next to his cousin so he could take her hand and feel for her pulse.

"I don't know," I said. "It felt like we were making some progress, and then she touched her head as if it hurt, and...she fainted."

Jake absorbed that information with a frown, then gently let go of Joanna's arm and laid it down on the ground. "Well, her pulse feels okay, but I'm still going to text Eleanor so she can make sure Joanna's really all right. Do you think you can help me carry Joanna inside? It's too cold to leave her lying out here like this."

"Yes," I replied at once, although I inwardly hoped that I wasn't being too optimistic. Joanna was pretty slender, but we'd still have to lug her up a set of steps just to get her onto the porch...and hope we didn't do anything to jar her too badly and make things worse than they already were.

Well, we'd deal with that when the time came. I stood and watched as Jake sent off a quick text to Eleanor, the Wilcox clan's healer, and took a quick inner survey to make sure I was feeling all right myself. But I didn't have a headache or anything, didn't feel woozy or weak. Whatever had affected Joanna didn't seem to have touched me at all.

And then I didn't really have time to worry, because Jake bent and got hold of Joanna by the shoulders, and I had to hurry over so I could pick up her feet. Taking careful, shuffling steps, we headed to the porch stairs and then slowly, awkwardly made our way up to the porch. Once there, we didn't have as hard a time going to the door, although we had to pause as Jake let go of her with one hand so he could open it.

From there, we staggered our way through the kitchen before we finally made it to the family room, where we gratefully laid her down on the couch. Through all of this, she hadn't stirred a bit, and the worry that had already threaded its way through me only grew in strength. What if something terrible had happened to her while she was attempting to break down the Freeman sisters' spell?

But then her eyes opened, and she stared at us for a second or two as if she couldn't quite figure out where she was. "What happened?"

Thank God. No slurring in those two words, and her dark eyes seemed bright and focused, if a bit confused.

"You fainted," I said. "Jake and I brought you inside. Eleanor's on her way over."

Joanna made a faint waving motion with one hand, as if to indicate that she didn't need to see the healer. "I'm fine."

"You think you're fine," Jake told her. "But I think it's a good idea to have her make sure."

Although her lips pressed together for a second or two, Joanna didn't look as though she intended to argue. "It was so strange...." she said, then let the words trail off.

"What was strange?" I asked. "Did you see something...sense something?"

"I'm not sure." She paused, then once again touched her fingers to her forehead, as if it still pained her. "It felt as if we were making some progress. And then it felt as if I'd just driven a car full speed into a brick wall. I guess that's when I passed out."

"I felt the same thing, too," I said. "I mean, that it felt as if we were getting somewhere. But I didn't seem to run into the same problem you did."

"Probably because your gift is stronger," she responded, now looking almost rueful, as if she should apologize for not being a stronger witch. "I don't know."

I opened my mouth to tell her I didn't think that was the issue, that some other dynamic must have been at work. However, the doorbell rang just then, and Jake hurried off to answer it. A moment later, he returned with Eleanor at his side. She was a slim woman in her late fifties, with streaks of gray in her dark hair and warm brown eyes that always made you feel immediately reassured.

Eleanor offered me a brief smile of acknowledgment but went to Joanna immediately. "How are you feeling, Joanna?" the healer asked.

"A little woozy, but I'm okay."

Apparently, Eleanor didn't intend to take Joanna's words at face value, because she laid her fingers against her wrist to take her pulse, and reached with her other hand to lay it against her cousin's forehead, checking on her temperature.

"Your vitals seem fine," she said. "Do you have a headache or weakness in any of your limbs?"

"No," Joanna replied. "I really feel okay now."

Her gaze slid past Eleanor to meet mine, and although Joanna didn't say anything out loud, she didn't have to. I got the distinct impression that she didn't want to mention the magic we were trying to perform, and so she expected me to keep my mouth shut, too.

Which was fine by me. I was still hoping we could keep Connor out of this, and so I was willing to stay silent for the time being.

Maybe Eleanor gave a very small lift of her shoulders. She looked over at Jake and me, but since neither of us appeared inclined to volunteer any more information, she probably decided that she might as well let it go.

"You seem fine," she said. "I couldn't pick up

on anything really wrong. But I think you should rest—and that means staying off your feet for the rest of the day. And no driving."

"I have to get home," Joanna protested.

"I'll drive your truck," Jake offered. "Addie can follow in her car."

Presented with that plan, she seemed to capitulate. "Okay. But I'm really fine."

"I'm sure you are," Eleanor said calmly. "But it never hurts to take precautions. Go home and rest, and if you experience any kind of dizziness or disorientation, call me right away."

"I will," Joanna replied with uncustomary meekness. It seemed clear to me that she didn't see the point in arguing with the healer.

Eleanor nodded. "Good. Then...take care of yourself, and I'll see you all at Connor's on Christmas Day."

Jake saw the healer to the door, then came right back to the family room. "Do you need to rest a while longer before we go?"

"Of course not," Joanna replied, now sounding irritated. "Like I said, I'm fine. Probably just some kind of magical blowback." She looked over at me. "How're you feeling?"

"Okay," I said. For some reason, I felt guilty about escaping the experience unscathed, even though I really didn't have any idea as to what had happened to us.

She absorbed that information, then slid her legs over the edge of the sofa and stood up. I couldn't detect any unsteadiness in her movements, but I was still glad that Jake would be driving her home.

I also hated to ask the question, even though I knew it needed to be said. "So...should I keep trying?"

"That seems like a very bad idea," Jake responded, but Joanna only shook her head, looking resigned.

"That's up to you, Addie," she said.

Just what I was afraid of.

6

Addie

I REALLY DIDN'T LIKE THE IDEA OF LEAVING Joanna alone in her house—it felt awfully isolated, even though she assured me that her closest neighbor was less than five minutes away—but I knew I didn't have much say in the matter. She kept reiterating that she was fine, and I had to accept her words at face value. Besides, she'd promised she would call Eleanor if she started to feel at all strange. There wasn't much else I—or Jake—could do.

So, I drove back to our house with him in the passenger seat of my little green Fiat and an uncomfortable silence stretching between us. I honestly didn't know what to say. Whatever had clapped back at Joanna hadn't affected me, for whatever reason. In my mind, that meant I needed to keep trying...but I had a feeling Jake had a very different opinion on the matter.

I pulled into the garage and parked my car next to his Wrangler, and we got out and went inside. By that point, it was almost noon, around time to think about scrounging some lunch. I wasn't hungry, though.

He went to the pantry and got out the little plastic bin that held Taffy's dog food, and scooped some into her bowl. She'd already followed us into the kitchen, knowing it was time for us to be putting together our own meal, and looked very disappointed as Jake instead leaned against the counter and sent me a searching look.

"I think you need to let it alone."

"Jake, nothing happened to me."

"This time."

Well, that comment was nothing more than the truth, so I couldn't think of a good way to contradict him. Yes, I was fine. That didn't mean I would be the next time.

"Leftovers for lunch?" I suggested, hoping I could distract him with food.

I should have known better. His brows drew together, and he said, "I think we need to talk to Connor."

Obviously, Jake wasn't going to let it go. I honestly didn't know why I was so dead set on keeping my brother out of the situation, except that it seemed to me if the Wilcox *primus* was brought into our mess, then he'd feel compelled to reach out to the Freeman *prima,* and I could see the whole thing spiraling out of control after that.

"What could Connor do, really?" I asked. "He's not a weather-worker. Getting him involved would just escalate everything."

"You don't know that," Jake replied. "And besides, he and Angela working together might be able to make this whole thing go away. I was willing to let you and Joanna try first, just because you two are the clan's weather witches, and it made a lot of sense to have you handle it. But obviously, that didn't work so well, so it's probably time to try something else."

I wished I could argue with him. Problem was, he had a point. Neither Connor nor Angela was a weather-worker, but when the two of them combined their powers, they could do almost anything. Or at least, it felt that way. Most of the time, they maintained a very low profile, but that didn't mean they couldn't pull off the kind of magical feats that most witches and warlocks only dreamed off.

"Maybe," I said. Knowing how sulky I must have sounded, I went over to him and wrapped my arms around his waist in the hope that he'd understand I wasn't trying to argue with him. It was only that I didn't like any of my current options.

At once, he returned the embrace, holding me close so I could revel in the warmth of his body against mine and the slow, steady beat of his heart as I laid my head against his chest. We stood that way for a long moment, until at last he bent and brushed his lips on the top of my head.

"We should eat," he said. "Then we can figure this out after lunch."

"Okay," I replied. Maybe sometime between then and now we'd be able to figure out an alternate solution to our problem, one that didn't involve reaching out to my brother for help.

Somehow, though, I guessed we wouldn't be that lucky.

Jake

As he'd guessed, Connor wasn't terribly happy to have been left out of the loop on a matter that impacted the whole clan—all of the Arizona witch families, when you got right down to it. Still, he hadn't wasted any time on recriminations. That just wasn't Connor's style.

"Send over this spell you told me about," he said. Somewhere in the background of the call,

Jake heard children's voices, but distantly, as though they were in another part of the house. "Angela and I will take a look at it and see if there's anything we can do. But otherwise, I'm probably going to need to talk to the Freeman *prima*. I assume Jeremy can get me her contact information."

Of course he could, but Jake hoped it wouldn't get to that point. "Um…probably," he allowed, and left it at that. "But I don't see what she can do. Lori Freeman told us her *prima's* gifts had nothing to do with weather-working."

"Maybe not, but she should still probably know what kind of mess a couple of her witches have gotten the rest of us into," Connor said. "I understand why Addie doesn't want to rat them out, but this is a lot bigger than whatever trouble they might be in with their *prima*."

"Well, you and Angela give it a try, and we'll go from there," Jake responded. "If you break their spell, then no harm, no foul, right?"

Connor didn't answer right away. Most likely, he was trying to decide which hole he wanted to pick in Jake's argument. When he spoke, however, he only said, "I suppose so. Lucas and Margot are taking the kids skating with Mia later this afternoon, and so Angela and I will have a couple of hours to ourselves. We'll give it a try once we're alone."

That offer was about all Jake could hope for. "Sounds great. I'll wait to hear from you, then."

"Okay. Talk to you later."

Connor ended the call, and Jake pulled the phone away from his ear and put it down on the coffee table. Addie sat on the couch, one leg tucked under her as she watched him anxiously.

"So…he's going for it?" she asked.

"Yes. He's just waiting until the kids are out of the house, and then he and Angela will see what they can do." Jake reached over and took her hand, and she wrapped her fingers around his. "See? It's all going to be fine."

She managed a smile, although he could tell that she didn't look completely convinced. However, she didn't argue, either. Like him, she knew about all they could do at that point was wait.

And sitting around the house didn't seem like a very good idea. If Connor and Angela were successful, it might mean that some weather could be moving in very soon. Jake figured that he and Addie might as well take advantage of the dry conditions while they could.

"Let's go out," he suggested, and she raised an eyebrow.

"'Out'? Where?"

"Just over to downtown," he said. "We can

walk around, look at the shops, maybe get a drink."

"Christmas Eve is tomorrow, you know," she pointed out. "Everything is going to be packed."

"Good," he said, and she sent him an incredulous look.

"It's good that it's going to be crazy crowded?"

"Yes," he replied. "It'll get you in the Christmas spirit. We already spent yesterday afternoon hanging around here while we were waiting for Lori Freeman to call you back. Wouldn't it be better to go out and get some fresh air instead of sitting here and wondering how it's going with Connor and Angela?"

For a second, Addie didn't respond. Then her mouth twisted into a lopsided smile, and she nodded.

"I suppose you're right," she said. "Let me brush my hair and touch up my face, and then we can go."

Personally, he didn't think her face needed any "touching up"—she always looked perfect to him —but he didn't bother to argue. Doing a bit of primping might make her feel better. Besides, she never took that long to get ready. For a very special occasion, she might spend the time to put on full makeup and use a curling iron to get some waves in her naturally straight hair, but otherwise, she was generally out the door with just some mascara and lip gloss.

While she went upstairs to get ready, Jake played with Taffy, rolling her tennis ball across the living room floor so the dog could chase it. He knew better than to throw the ball in the house—he'd once nearly broken a lamp doing that very thing—but it was enough to keep the dog occupied and, he hoped, make her a little less upset by being left alone for a chunk of the afternoon.

Addie came back down, hair lying sleek and shining over her shoulders, and smiled to see him playing keep-away with Taffy's tennis ball. The smile lit up her face and made her look far more relaxed, and Jake hoped she'd remain that way for the rest of the afternoon. Yes, the Freeman witches' spell was a problem, but he didn't want her to take the weight of the world on her shoulders, especially not during the holidays, when she should be trying to relax and enjoy herself.

They put on their coats, and Addie swung her purse over one shoulder. After petting Taffy and promising her that they would be home for dinner, Jake let them out, and closed and locked the door. It was a brisk, bright day, with a sharp wind blowing from the northwest. A wind like that should have been carrying some weather with it, but he knew that wasn't going to happen unless Connor and Angela managed to brute-force their way past the spell that kept the storms trapped on the western coast.

"Any last-minute errands you need to run?" Jake asked as they headed toward downtown, and Addie shook her head.

"Not really. I shopped like a madwoman last week so I wouldn't have to go near the stores this week."

There hadn't been even the slightest hint of accusation in her tone, but Jake still found himself saying, "Sorry about that."

She reached up with a gloved hand to push a stray strand of hair away from her face. "Don't be. It feels good to get out. And really, since there isn't any shopping I *have* to do, it takes all the pressure off. We can just relax and have fun."

"And maybe have a glass of wine?"

That question made her laugh outright. "Ah, now I see your ulterior motive. Well, if we can find a seat somewhere, sure."

Hearing her laugh made him feel better about the situation. At least she wasn't so stressed out that she couldn't allow herself to relax a bit. It would do both of them good. Also, there was no need to feel guilty about getting a little R&R, since Jake had called Joanna after lunch to see how she was feeling, and it sounded as though she'd bounced right back from her fainting spell.

"Honestly, I feel like an idiot sitting here with my feet up, doing nothing," she'd groused.

"You still need to take it easy, just like Eleanor told you to do," he'd replied.

"I know. And I am. But tomorrow, all bets are off."

Since he'd known better than to argue with her, he'd only said that maybe it would be better to check with the healer before she decided to paint the barn or something, and Joanna had chuckled and told him she'd take it under advisement, and that she'd see him and Addie at the Christmas potluck.

But since Joanna seemed fine, Jake didn't see any reason not to grab a drink somewhere while he and Addie were out. If, as she'd warned, they could even find a place to sit down.

As predicted, the stores were crowded with people doing last-minute shopping. Having no set destination helped, because they could simply duck out of the shops that were too impacted and move on to the next place. And although Vino Loco, the wine bar up on Birch Street, was full as well, they lucked out and were able to grab a couple of seats at one end of the bar when the couple who'd been sitting there got up and left.

"See?" he said as they lifted their glasses of malbec and toasted one another. "Nothing to it."

"If you were your cousin Lucas, I'd say there

was something a little more than plain old good timing at work," Addie replied before taking a sip of her wine. "But I have to admit that this was easier than I thought it would be."

"Maybe that's a sign."

Her brows lifted. "I'd like to think so. But...."

The words trailed off, and she sipped some more wine. However, Jake guessed she was thinking that the situation with the Freeman witches' spell probably wouldn't be solved quite so easily. He didn't say anything, however, because with the way they were packed in at the bar, with another couple less than a foot away from where they perched on their barstools, it wasn't the sort of setup where they could share confidences about magic and spells.

In a way, that was better. They could chat instead about dinner the next night at his parents' house, and about the big potluck at Connor and Angela's place on Christmas Day, and about the outing they had planned with Jeremy and Sloane to drive out to Winslow and have dinner at the Turquoise Room at the La Posada Hotel on Boxing Day. It was the sort of conversation any couple out and about a few days before Christmas might have shared, and for a minute here and there, he found himself almost forgetting about the shadow that hung over all their heads.

Eventually, though, the day stretched past five

o'clock, and they turned toward home. Jake's phone had been suspiciously silent that whole time, and troubling thoughts began to creep into his mind. What if Connor and Angela had run into the same barrier that had made Joanna faint? What if they were both passed out on the floor of their big house in Forest Highlands?

As best he could, Jake kept those doubts to himself. He and Addie had shared a mellow, relaxing afternoon, and he didn't want to do anything that might shatter the fragile equilibrium they'd managed to create. When they got home, they didn't bother to take off their coats, but took Taffy out for her evening walk.

And still no phone call.

He was just about to suggest that they start thinking about ordering in dinner when his phone finally buzzed. By that point, he and Addie were sitting on the couch in the family room, the dog perched near their feet and gazing at them expectantly. It wasn't quite six, but close enough to supper time that she clearly thought she might be able to importune them into feeding her early.

At once, Jake scooped the phone out of his pocket and touched the screen to accept the call without even bothering to look at the number on the display.

"Hey, Jake."

Connor, his voice tired. Well, at least those

dark fantasies had been nothing more than trouble-borrowing, but at the same time, Jake had a feeling he was about to hear some bad news. Otherwise, his cousin would have sounded a hell of a lot more upbeat.

"Hi, Connor," he replied. Next to him, Addie straightened and uncrossed her legs, her gaze sharpening as she looked in his direction.

"Well, it didn't work."

He'd already gathered that much but made himself ask, "What happened?"

"A whole lot of nothing. I mean, the spell seemed straightforward to us. We thought it would be easy enough to pull a thread and have the whole thing unravel. But no matter what we tried, we couldn't get it broken down."

Hell. Jake ran his free hand through his hair, mind working furiously. Problem was, he couldn't think of a single piece of advice to offer, not a damn bit of insight as to how they could undo that horrible spell. "Are you and Angela okay?"

"We're fine," Connor said. "We didn't have any blowback, if that's what you're worried about. No, it was just the two of us beating our heads against this thing for the past two hours."

"Sorry."

"No reason to be sorry. It's part of our job." Connor paused then before adding, "But I really think it's time we try to reach out to the Freeman *prima*."

The one thing Addie had been trying to avoid. He opened his mouth to offer some sort of delaying remark, but she gestured toward the phone, obviously asking if she could talk to her brother.

Jake knew there was no point in arguing with her, so he pulled the iPhone away from his ear and handed it over to her.

"Hey, Connor," she said. "I heard what you said to Jake. Can we just give it a little more time? I mean, it's almost Christmas. Why dump this on the Freeman *prima* now? A few more dry days aren't going to hurt anything. You can talk to her after the holiday."

Because she was holding the phone slightly away from her ear, Jake was able to hear Connor's reply. "I suppose you have a point. Sure, I can hold off for a couple of days. But I'm going to have to talk to her eventually."

"That's fine," she replied. "I know we can't let this go on forever. I just think that waiting until after Christmas is a good idea."

"All right. But don't do anything crazy."

"I won't. See you on Thursday."

"See you then."

The call ended there, and Addie handed the phone back to Jake. A small gleam in her eyes seemed to tell him that her reassurances about not doing anything crazy might have been a bit of a prevarication.

Should he push it?

Oh, what the hell.

"What are you thinking, Addie?"

"I don't know yet," she replied. "For the moment, I'm fresh out of ideas. All I know is that I just bought us a little breathing room."

Although that answer wasn't quite enough to put all his worries to rest, at least Jake guessed she didn't have any immediate plans she wanted to put into action. He had no doubt that her mind was humming away, however, doing its best to find something they might all have missed.

"Fair enough," he said. "Let's order some take-out. I was thinking Indian, since we're going to be filling up on holiday food for the next couple of days."

"Sounds good."

He called in the order, then went into the kitchen so he could give Taffy her dinner. While he was occupied with that task, Addie got up from the couch and busied herself with getting the table set. He plucked a bottle of wine from the countertop rack and carried it into the dining room, pausing long enough to get the corkscrew from the sideboard.

Neither one of them spoke, which was probably just as well. Jake figured they could discuss the problem of the Freeman witches over dinner...or maybe not. He'd take his cues from Addie.

She was looking particularly gorgeous in her dark green sweater, hair shining like polished mahogany against the soft cashmere. The tourmaline and rock crystal pendant she'd bought for herself in Jerome—one of Angela's creations—dangled from her throat as she bent to light one of the candles at the center of the table. Looking at her, Jake wondered if there had ever been a more amazing woman in the world.

He doubted it. A warmth that only had a little to do with desire flooded him then, and he wondered what the hell he'd been waiting for. The perfect moment to ask the question didn't exist— or rather, any moment he asked her would be the perfect one, because she would be a part of it.

"Um, I need to run up to the bedroom and get something," he said. "If the delivery guy shows up, you can tip him, but the order is prepaid."

"Sure," Addie said, looking a little confused by the request. Most likely, she was wondering what in the world he needed from the bedroom when they were just about to sit down to dinner.

But she didn't stop him, and so he hurried upstairs, dug the ring box out of his nightstand drawer, and stowed it in his jeans pocket. Just as he was coming back down, the doorbell rang, and so he was able to go ahead and answer it before Addie had even emerged from the dining room.

Then it was all about getting the food transferred from the takeout containers to the bowls and platters she'd set out on the dining room table—and trying not to trip over Taffy, who was running around in excitement, tail wagging furiously at all the exciting smells. But eventually, they were sitting down in their respective seats, with the dog perched between them on the rug as she waited for her chance to beg for some tasty morsels.

Jake poured wine for both of them. The ring box felt odd, smashed up against his hip bone, but he ignored the discomfort. He didn't know exactly when he would ask the question, figuring that he'd just go with the flow and decide when the time was right. All he knew was that it would happen sometime this evening, no matter what. Whatever happened with breaking the Freeman witches' weather spell, he wanted at least one part of their holiday to create the happy memories they both wanted this Christmas.

They talked about Addie's return to school after the winter holidays were over, and possible plans to head south during spring break to soak up some warmer weather in Tucson, or maybe Tubac. Things had been fairly quiet at Trident

Enterprises lately, and so Jake didn't foresee any problems with taking a few days or even a week off. At another time, he might have been disappointed that his project wasn't seeing the activity he'd hoped for, but at the moment, he found he didn't care as much as he thought he would. After all, they'd found Addie and Sloane—and all the people who'd been caught up in Project Daedalus. If the Trident team had located so many witches and warlocks individually, he would have thought the project a huge success. Should it matter that fourteen of them had been located at the same time?

Probably not.

"I can't get too carried away with vacations, though," Addie said. "In between all this other stuff, I have to study for the GRE."

Right. He'd almost forgotten about that, since he'd had no desire to continue to grad school after he got his bachelor's degree, but passing the test was necessary for her to get into the library science program at Northern Pines.

"Okay, then just three or four days in Tucson," he said with a grin.

A smile of her own flickered around her full lips. "We'll see." She paused there and looked down at her nearly empty plate. Everything except a small bite of naan had been eaten. "I guess we're about done. Unless you want some more butter chicken."

"No, I'm fine," he replied. Should he ask her now, before they got up from the table? Or wait until they'd moved into the family room to watch TV?

Better in the dining room, he thought. At least in there, candles flickered from the table and the Tiffany-style chandelier overhead had been dimmed to a warm glow. It was a much more romantic setting than the family room, with Addie's books scattered across the coffee table and one of Taffy's dog beds taking up space next to the sofa.

"But...." he began, and she tilted her head at him, clearly wondering why he would want to delay getting up from the table.

"But...?"

"I—I wanted to ask you something," he said. Was he supposed to go down on one knee? That was how this sort of scene tended to be portrayed in books and movies, and yet, he had a feeling if he attempted that sort of display, Addie would probably burst out laughing.

Or maybe not. Something in her expression had gone still, as if she had some inkling of what he was about to say. However, she sat there quietly, inviting him to go on, and that silent acceptance told him he was doing exactly the right thing.

"I can't imagine my life without you, Addie," he told her. "These last six months…they've been perfect. Because you're perfect."

Her lips parted, but then she closed her mouth again, as though she understood that she needed to let him say the words, that she shouldn't interrupt.

"I don't want this to ever end," he said. With one hand, he reached in his pocket and drew out the ring box, then slowly opened it with his other. The diamond inside glittered in the reflection of the candles, the warm flames awakening brilliant sparks from deep within. "Addie Grant, will you be my wife?"

For a second, her eyes widened. But then she nodded. "Yes, Jake. Oh, yes."

Although his hands wanted to shake, he somehow extricated the ring from the box and managed to slip it on her left hand. To his relief, it fit perfectly. He'd measured the inner circumference of the turquoise ring she always wore on her other hand and had taken that measurement to the jeweler, but he hadn't known whether she wore the same size on both hands.

She stared down at the ring, as if awed by the diamond that sparkled within its platinum setting. "It's—it's beautiful, Jake. I love it."

That was all, but he could tell from the glow in her eyes and the warmth in her voice that he'd chosen the perfect ring for her. He got up from his chair and went to her, and she rose as well, her hands reaching for his so she could hold on tightly.

Their lips met, and the spices he tasted on her mouth were an echo of the first kiss they'd shared after eating a meal not so different from this one. Back then, he'd held the hidden hope in his heart that they might be able to come to a moment like this, but he hadn't known that life with her could be as wonderful as it had turned out to be. Sometimes, dreams were a pale reflection of reality.

When they parted, she smiled up at him. "I think Christmas might be kind of a letdown after this."

His fingers tightened on hers. "No, it'll be wonderful, because it'll be our first Christmas together."

She gave a single nod, as if absorbing the idea. Then she went on her tiptoes and kissed him very gently on the cheek. "You know what? I think you may be right."

No mention of the Freeman witches' bungled spell, or of the duty that had fallen to her because no one else seemed able to manage the task in question. Jake couldn't help but be relieved by that; he wanted this moment to remain as it was, without any outside worries or troubles to inter-fere with the little bubble of perfection they'd created for themselves.

If any of those thoughts crossed Addie's mind, she didn't give voice to them. She only tugged at his hand, her gaze drifting upward, and he was all too happy to go along.

After all, holding her in his arms would only seal the promise they'd just made to one another.

7

Addie

THE ENGAGEMENT RING WAS A STRANGE, beautiful weight on my finger. I wasn't used to wearing rings on my left hand, but I also knew I wouldn't take it off except to clean it. As I stared down at the diamond in the bright light from the fixture mounted above the bathroom mirror, I couldn't help being mesmerized by the sparks of brilliance that seemed to emanate from the stone every time I moved. Glints of blue and rose and pale yellow, all sparkling up and down the spectrum from the intricate facets deep within.

I wouldn't allow myself to think about how much it must have cost. Not that I knew very much about diamonds—i.e., nothing at all—but I had to believe that a stone so clear and bright and perfectly cut must have been very expensive.

He can afford it, I told myself, which was only the truth. I didn't think a single Wilcox was hurting for money, and Jake was no exception… especially since the glorious restored Victorian house we shared had already been paid for. When all you had to worry about was the utility bills and your food and maybe a few miscellaneous expenses like car registration or property tax, that Wilcox stipend of five grand a month could stretch a really long way.

We'd come home after going to the movies so we could both get changed for dinner at his parents' house that Christmas Eve. The whole day, I'd been acutely aware of the ring's sparkle on my finger, even though I didn't think anyone else had paid any real attention to it, including the girl who'd taken our ticket stubs at the theater. No, I was just self-conscious because the ring was new…and so was my entire situation.

Or at least, it felt that way. Yes, Jake and I had been living together for nearly six months, so on the one hand, nothing much had really changed. Except now we'd made a pledge to spend the rest of our lives together, had made real the implicit agreement we'd shared all along.

He'd told me that his mother made sort of a big deal about Christmas Eve, so I knew I had to

make a special effort to get ready. That was why I
wore the only skirt I owned, a narrow black wool
piece I'd found on sale at Macy's, and black high-
heeled boots I'd bought on Sloane's advice, even
though I'd thought to myself that I very much
doubted I'd wear them more than a couple of
times a year. A red cashmere cardigan with a lace-
trimmed black tank underneath, and I was probably more put together than I'd ever been in my
life.

I didn't have any jewelry that went well with
red, other than my old standby silver hoop
earrings, so I put them on and gave my hair
another quick brushing. In a way, the lack of any
other rings only made the diamond Jake had given
me stand out that much more, and I liked the
effect.

Since he was waiting for me downstairs, I
didn't linger, but only scooped up my purse from
where I'd left it sitting at the foot of the bed and
headed down to the family room. He had his feet
up on the coffee table and was absently scrolling
through the offerings on Netflix, although he
turned off the TV and set down the remote as
soon as I entered the room.

"You look incredible," he said.

A warm flush touched my cheeks. Yes, it was
flattering to have him stare at me like that, but I
still had a hard time with compliments. Self-

consciously, I ran a hand down the side of my skirt, smoothing away an imaginary wrinkle. "It's not too much?"

At once, he came over to me and gave me a quick kiss—on the cheek, as if he knew better than to mess up the gloss I'd applied just a few minutes earlier. "No, you look perfect."

"You're looking pretty fine yourself," I said, which was only the truth. He wore a dark green button-up shirt and nice new jeans, with a charcoal gray tweed jacket on top of everything.

He tugged at one lapel. "I feel like a college professor in this thing."

"No, it's great," I told him, then added, "Trust me—none of my professors looks anything like you."

"What a relief."

I chuckled, although I had a feeling he was being at least halfway serious. But it was a quarter after six, which meant we needed to get going. Taffy had already been fed, and wore the resigned expression of a dog who knew she was going to be abandoned for the next couple of hours. Bringing her along wasn't really an option, not when Theresa, Jake's mother, had a big fluffy calico cat who ruled the roost and would have made her feelings known if we'd had the temerity to bring a dog to Christmas Eve dinner.

So, we petted Taffy and told her we wouldn't

be gone all that long, and got our coats before heading out to the garage. The night air was almost painfully cold, and hard, bright stars shone down from a moonless sky. All those stars seemed to exist only to remind me of how clear that sky was, of how I couldn't find a single cloud to dim their brightness. The whole day, Jake and I had studiously avoided the topic of the Freeman witches' spell, but the problem had continued to lurk in the back of my mind, never allowing me to be totally at ease. And yes, I'd told him I wanted to put the issue aside until after Christmas, and yet I knew doing so wasn't entirely feasible. My brain had continued to pick at the problem in the background, although I hadn't been able to devise anything close to a workable solution.

Theresa and Raymond Wilcox's house was located in a pretty, wooded area south of I-40 called Country Club Estates. Their home was the sort of place I wished I'd grown up in, a big two-story with four bedrooms and a large backyard ringed with trees. Almost from the first time I walked into the house, I felt welcome there, although I didn't know whether that was due to the sort of friendly, overstuffed furniture Theresa had used in her decor, or because Jake's parents had done everything they could to make me a part of their family from the beginning.

Still, I couldn't help being a little nervous as

the two of us stepped into the entry that evening. We hadn't told anyone about our engagement, figuring we'd be seeing Jake's immediate family on Christmas Eve, and Connor and Angela and most of the Wilcoxes the following day. Most likely, everyone had viewed our getting engaged as a foregone conclusion, and so we wouldn't be surprising anyone. Even so, I knew I wanted to get the announcement over with as soon as possible.

Not that we actually had to do anything so formal. The moment we came into the house, Theresa and Raymond appeared and gave us both hugs. Then she looked down and grabbed my hand. "What's this?"

"What does it look like, Mom?" Jake observed dryly.

"It looks like an engagement ring," she returned, mouth twitching. Like her sons, she had dark eyes and hair, although hers had an interesting streak of gray that ran from her right temple down to the end of her shoulder-length bob. I hoped Jake's hair would turn gray the same way, because it was a very cool effect.

"Congratulations," Raymond said. "I think this calls for a drink. We've got a bottle of rosé open—come on into the family room."

Relieved that the moment had passed so easily, I followed him into the family room, with Jake and his mother behind me. A leather-covered wine bucket sat on the coffee table, with the afore-mentioned bottle of rosé chilling in it. Since the space was located next to the kitchen, the air was filled with the scent of homemade spiced cranberry relish and roasted potatoes and all sorts of other goodies. I tried not to be too obvious about the way I inhaled all those wonderful aromas, and hoped my stomach wouldn't growl. We'd held off on ordering snacks during the movie because we knew we would be eating a big dinner afterward, but I was pretty hungry by that point.

Raymond poured wine for all of us, and he held up his glass in a toast. "A long and wonderful life together, you two," he said. "If you're even only half as happy as Theresa and I have been, then you'll be doing well."

"Oh," Theresa said, blushing, then stopped, as if she wasn't quite sure what else to add.

"To a long and wonderful life," Jake echoed, and we all clinked our glasses together and took a sip. The rosé was cool and tart, and surprisingly refreshing.

"Have you settled on a date?" Theresa asked then.

Jake and I exchanged a glance. We honestly hadn't, although we knew that, practically speaking, we wouldn't have the wedding until after I'd graduated in late May.

"Um…probably June?" I said, ending on a rising inflection so he'd know I was asking for his input.

"Right," he chimed in. "Probably toward the end of the month. We'll figure it out—we have six months."

"Six months isn't that long when you're planning a wedding," his mother told him, a slight frown pulling at her brows.

"Even a Wilcox wedding?" I asked.

That question erased the frown, and her lips curved in a smile. "Well, all right—we are pretty good at getting things to go smoothly. Still, I wouldn't put it off for too long."

"We won't," Jake assured her. "Once we're past Christmas, then Addie and I will sit down with a calendar and figure it out, and we can go from there."

She opened her mouth to reply but was interrupted by the arrival of Jeremy and Sloane, who'd paused at the entry to the family room to take in the scene before them. "What, you couldn't even wait until we got here before you started drinking?" he quipped.

"We're celebrating," his mother replied in mock-severe tones. "Jake and Addie are engaged!"

Of course, that announcement was followed by more congratulations and hugs. Sloane seized my hand so she could give the engagement ring a critical eye. Being Sloane, she was looking absolutely gorgeous in a dark green wrap dress and boots very similar to mine, with a heavy silver collar necklace around her throat.

"Good choice," she said approvingly as she inspected the ring. "Very classy."

"I'm glad you like it," Jake said dryly.

"When's the big day?" Jeremy asked.

"We're not sure yet," I replied, glad I could change the subject from my engagement ring. "But probably sometime in June."

That answer got a nod, and then Raymond poured wine for Jeremy and Sloane so we could toast all over again. After that, Theresa shooed us into the dining room, saying it was time to get dinner on the table. Jake and Jeremy piped up then, offering to help, but we all knew that was mostly ritual. I'd learned that Theresa would have Raymond help but didn't expect any of the rest of us to lift a finger—we were guests.

So, we trooped into the dining room and took the seats that had been designated for us, since Theresa had gone all out and used place cards with fancy calligraphy to let everyone know where they needed to sit. Not too long afterward, she and Raymond started bringing in the food—smoked turkey, homemade cranberry relish, roasted potatoes, pan-roasted brussels sprouts.

Everything looked delicious, and tasted even

better. We talked about the upcoming wedding, with Theresa suggesting various venues, and Jake either agreeing or saying he wasn't sure whether they would work or not. About all I could do was nod at appropriate times and hope I'd remember half of what they were discussing, since even after six months in Flagstaff, I was far from familiar with all the restaurants and hotels and other places that might be suitable for hosting a wedding.

During this conversation, I noted Jeremy sending a couple of furtive glances toward Sloane, as if he feared she might catch wedding fever and start pressing him to formalize their relationship. However, she only looked interested and engaged, and not at all jealous, and so I thought he was probably worried over nothing. They'd only been together for three months, after all, although I guessed they'd be taking that big next step sometime in the coming year. Or maybe not. She seemed happy enough with their current arrangement, and maybe didn't see the need to get married until they got serious about having a family, or at least until she was finished with college.

At any rate, it turned out to be an easygoing evening that went by much more quickly than I'd thought it would. After dinner, we took a break to exchange presents in the living room, with a big wood fire burning in the hearth and holiday music playing softly in the background. Sloane and Jeremy got me a gorgeous pair of silver and green tourmaline earrings—"I thought they'd match that necklace you wear all the time," she told me—and Theresa and Raymond gave me a fabulous leather messenger bag for hauling my books around. The two brothers continued their tradition of gifting each other T-shirts from local breweries, while Jake and I gave Sloane a gift certificate for a spa day, and all of the younger generation chipped in to buy the parents a weekend at a resort down in Scottsdale.

"It'll be good for getting away while the rest of us are being snowed in," Jeremy told them, and Jake sent a quick, worried look in my direction. That was the first time during the evening that the subject of the weather had even come up, and I could tell he was worried about how I would react.

Luckily, I was able to smile at his brother's comment and act as though nothing about it had bothered me in the slightest. Sure, I experienced an inner twinge, but I didn't think anyone noticed anything. However, Jeremy's words started worry bubbling inside me once again, even though I'd managed to put my concerns aside up until that point.

But the moment passed, and we headed back to the dining room for pie and coffee for those of us who wanted it. The get-together broke up soon after that and we made our goodbyes…although not for long, since we'd all be seeing each other the next day at the big Wilcox potluck.

Jake was mostly quiet during our drive back to the house. Just as he was pulling into the garage, however, he said, "I don't think Jeremy meant anything by that comment."

"I know he didn't," I replied. "It's okay. I've known Jeremy long enough now that I've kind of figured out that he doesn't have much of a filter."

A chuckle. "No, not really. It's definitely not as though Sloane has to use her mind-reading ability to see what's in his head."

That was for sure. Then again, I knew Sloane wouldn't do such a thing, because she'd told me not long after she moved in with Jeremy that she didn't use her gift to peer into other people's minds unless she absolutely had to. It wasn't as though she went around sneaking peeks all over the place just for the hell of it. And although I really hadn't suspected her of doing such a thing, it was still good to get that kind of confirmation from her.

We went inside and were greeted by the dog, who seemed ecstatic at our return. After letting her outside to do her business, we wandered into the living room. We'd left off the lights on the Christmas tree since it hadn't seemed safe to have them lit when we weren't home, but Jake went over to the tree and bent so he could turn them on. At once, hundreds of little white fairy lights came to life, softly illuminating the space.

"That's better," he said, and turned back toward me.

Our eyes met. Although neither of us said anything, we both moved at the same time, going to one another so we could fall into an embrace, his mouth hungry on mine, tasting of wine and cherry pie. Heat rushed through me, and I pressed my body against his, wanting more.

No words were necessary as he slipped his hand into mine and led me upstairs to the bedroom. Once there, we pulled at each other's clothes almost recklessly, throwing our holiday finery onto the carpet so we could get into bed that much more quickly. His hands on me then, stroking me, making me moan at the ripples of pleasure flooding through my body. The air in the room was just slightly chilly, but we were both so heated with need that neither of us cared too much.

We shifted so we could both taste one another, could each give our own gifts of pleasure. Even as I shuddered from the orgasm Jake had sent shivering through me, he moved again, this time pulling me down on top of him, his hands moving over my breasts, caressing the sensitive flesh, making me moan even more loudly as he thrust deeper and deeper.

By that time, we'd grown accustomed to one another's rhythms, knew how to fall in sync with each other by instinct. Building, building...and then I cried out yet again when another orgasm hit, my moans blending with Jake's as the climax hit him as well. We stayed that way, locked together, fingers entwined, until our breathing began to settle and I finally slid off him.

"I love you," I whispered, and he pulled me close to his body, heated from our exertions.

"I love you," he replied. "You're the best present I could ever have."

I smiled, and allowed myself to enjoy our warmth.

Soon enough, I feared, I would have to venture out into the cold, and try to fix what the Freeman witches had broken. Not on Christmas, because our day would be full, but I knew I couldn't allow this weather to continue. I wanted a white Christmas, true, although I knew it was more than that. There was a pattern to things, to how the world was supposed to work, and Lori and Lisa Freeman had disrupted that pattern. Unwittingly, of course, but still.

I only hoped I could weave that pattern back together again, and make it whole.

8

Jake

CHRISTMAS MORNING. THE ONLY GIFT HE'D really needed was waking up with Addie next to him, but he had to admit that it was more fun than he'd anticipated to sit down in the living room with his coffee as she played Santa and brought over the various packages and gift bags that were his presents.

"All this for me?" he asked, looking over the respectable pile on the floor next to where he sat.

A rueful dimple showed in one cheek. "Maybe I went a little overboard. This was just the first Christmas...." The words trailed off there, and she pulled in a breath. "This was the first Christmas where I didn't have to worry about how much things cost."

He reached over and took her hand, squeezing her fingers gently. Usually, she was very careful with her money, even when she didn't have to be, and so this overwhelming evidence of her love for him moved him more than he could say.

She seemed to understand, because she nodded and then grabbed a box and handed it to him. "You'd better start opening these," she said with a smile that seemed just a little forced. "Otherwise, we're going to be late to the potluck."

"It doesn't start until two," he pointed out, and her smile relaxed into something a little more natural, even as a glint appeared in her smoky gray-green eyes.

"Maybe, but that's a lot of presents."

He shook his head and tore off the wrapping paper from the box he held. Inside was a gorgeous Swiss Army knife, far more elaborate than the one he currently owned. "This is amazing, Addie," he said.

"I thought it seemed pretty cool. But you have to give me a penny for it, or it's bad luck. At least, that's what I've heard."

Jake didn't know where that old tradition had come from, but he figured it was better not to argue. Unfortunately, he had on an old pair of flannel pajama bottoms and not his jeans. He was just about to tell Addie that he needed to run upstairs to get a penny when he remembered there was always some loose change floating around in the drawers of the coffee table. So, he extracted a penny and gave it to her, and she slipped it into the pocket of the fleece robe she was wearing.

"Now you open one," he told her, and she went over to the tree and picked up a silver foil gift bag with candy canes all over it. Since he sucked at wrapping presents, he'd long ago switched completely to using gift bags.

She took the bag and came over and sat down next to him, then unwrapped the tissue paper from the box inside. "A Kindle?" she said, and turned the box over in her hand, as if she wasn't entirely sure what to do with it.

"I was hoping maybe that would keep you from leaving books all over the house."

In response, she stuck out her tongue at him, and he leaned over and pulled her close so he could give her a big coffee-flavored kiss. She gasped and then laughed, and he kissed her again before letting go so she could get up to fetch another present.

By the time they were done, he had a new pair of hiking boots and several shirts and a new wallet, along with a set of *Red Dwarf* DVDs and various assorted other items he'd mentioned in passing that he might like, never dreaming that Addie would go out and buy all of them for him. He hadn't been quite so extravagant when purchasing gifts for her, but he'd known that Jeremy and Sloane were getting her those green tourmaline earrings, and he'd commissioned Angela to make a ring to match the pendant Addie had bought all those months ago in Jerome.

"It's gorgeous," she said as she slipped it onto her finger, then held out her hand so she could admire the cool green flicker of the tourmaline against her skin. "You've showered me in jewels this year."

"I don't think two rings exactly constitutes a 'shower,'" he replied. "But I'm glad you like it."

"I love it. And I'm so glad I'm wearing that green sweater I found at Dillard's last week. It'll be perfect."

Which it was. The Wilcox potluck tended to be a more casual sort of get-together than his mother's Christmas Eve dinner, and so once they were done with their showers, he and Addie both got dressed in jeans. But hers were the skinny kind that showed off her long, slender legs, and she wore the jeans tucked into tall brown boots, so the combination with the green cashmere sweater was still pretty striking.

After they got into his Wrangler, he looked over at her. She appeared calm enough, but a certain tension in the set of her jaw told him she was still probably worried about the prospect of facing the extended family.

"It's going to be great," he said. "You already know a lot of the people who'll be there. And Ethan and Natalie will be coming."

That comment seemed to relax her slightly. She buckled her seatbelt and said, "Oh, they are? The last time I talked to Natalie, she sounded as if she still wasn't sure."

"Well, Laurel talked her into it. I guess Natalie was making noises about how she wasn't sure whether they should go, since they weren't really Wilcoxes. But Laurel told her they were pretty much honorary members of the clan, and that seemed to convince Natalie."

Addie absorbed that information, a faint smile playing around her lips. "You Wilcoxes have taken in a lot of us strays."

"Not that many," he replied as he backed the Jeep out of the driveway and pointed it toward Milton Avenue, Flagstaff's main drag. "And you don't really count."

An eyebrow arched. "I don't?"

He grimaced. Talk about sticking your foot in it. "What I meant was, you're a Wilcox, so I don't think you really count as a 'stray.' And otherwise, it's just Sloane and Ethan and Natalie in terms of orphan witches we've given shelter."

The amused glint in her eyes disappeared. "You forgot Randall Lenz."

Actually, Jake hadn't. He'd just thought it was

probably better not to mention the man. Lenz did a damn good job of staying out of Addie's orbit, but she still couldn't pretend he wasn't around. At least there was no chance of crossing paths at the potluck; Connor had told Jake that he'd invited the former federal agent to the get-together out of politeness, since he didn't want to think of even Randall Lenz having to sit at home alone on Christmas. But Lenz had told him he was going back to New York to visit his mother for the holidays, and so he was safely three thousand miles away.

Too bad he couldn't stay there. Jake pushed aside the uncharitable thought—after all, he and Addie might still be prisoners in the SED facility if it weren't for Lenz switching sides and helping to get them and the rest of the test subjects out of there—but he was forced to admit that he doubted he would ever warm up to the guy.

Which was fine. Just because he'd done them a good turn didn't mean they had to be best friends.

"I guess I did forget about him," Jake said, figuring it was better to offer a little white lie rather than state that he'd been trying to avoid making any mention of the man.

Addie didn't comment, only nodded and then turned her head to look out the window. Not that there was much to see, since this stretch of Milton Road wasn't exactly picturesque. The parking lot at the Target was a wasteland, a contrast to how packed it would have been even the day before.

Ten more minutes, and he was hunting for a place to park on Connor and Angela's street—no mean feat, since the Wilcoxes had descended en masse, and it looked as though several of the neighbors were also hosting Christmas Day parties.

Eventually, though, Jake located a spot around the corner and halfway down the block. Since all they had to bring was their contribution to the potluck—an apple pie based on a recipe Addie's mother had taught her—it wasn't too much of an inconvenience to carry it over to the house. Thank God the Wilcoxes had long ago given up doing a gift exchange at these things.

As soon as they opened the front door, a rush of noise greeted them—voices chattering away, various *clinks* and *clanks* coming from the kitchen, little kids laughing, and underneath it all, a New Age-y version of "Hark, the Herald Angels Sing." At his side, Addie quailed slightly and clutched the pie she held even more tightly.

Jake gave her arm a reassuring squeeze and pushed into the fray. From either side came calls of greeting, and he responded with a "hello" and a smile and a wave, while Addie gamely tried to do the same. Eventually, they made it to the dining room, where she went ahead and put the pie down on the section of the sideboard designated for desserts.

Connor and Angela came out of the kitchen, offering their own greetings and some quick hugs.

"I know it seems like bedlam," Connor said, gaze focused on his sister. "But really, it's not so bad. Grab a drink—I think Jeremy and Sloane are over in the family room."

"Great," Addie replied. "We'll go find them."

"But we'll get a drink first," Jake put in. She definitely looked like she needed one.

Connor grinned but didn't have a chance to reply, since someone was calling his name. Angela shot them a smile of her own and then hurried off in response to a chorus of "Mom" emanating from somewhere in the living room.

"Drinks," Jake said firmly, and guided Addie over to the long folding table that had been set up as an impromptu bar. There was wine and beer and a variety of mixers, along with punch in both leaded and unleaded varieties. He figured wine would probably be safest, and so he filled two plastic cups with a local red blend and handed one to her.

She took it from him gratefully and sipped some wine. "Thanks," she said.

"I figured you could use it. Now, let's go find Sloane and Jeremy."

As Connor had said, they were in the family

room, Jeremy with a beer bottle in one hand, and Sloane holding a plastic cup of wine. After sharing greetings, Sloane said, "Man, am I glad to see you guys. I feel like I'm lost in a forest of Wilcoxes."

Jake chuckled, but Addie replied quite seriously, "Well, we're Wilcoxes, too, you know."

Sloane wrinkled her nose. "I know that intellectually, but it doesn't quite feel the same."

"Well, I think we got more people than usual because the weather is good," Jeremy observed.

At once, Addie's expression fell. "We're working on it, okay?"

"I didn't mean it that way," Jeremy said, even as Sloane shot him an exasperated glance. "It's just that a lot of the time, it's snowing on Christmas Day and people don't want to travel."

"Not helping, Jeremy," Jake told him, seeing the way Addie's mouth tightened at his remark.

"It's okay—" she began, but he shook his head.

"The weather is off limits," he said, and Sloane shot a warning look at her companion.

"Hey, what time did you want to meet at your place tomorrow?" she asked.

"Eleven," Jake replied. Yes, the change in subject was so obvious, he could have seen it from space, but he was glad for the interruption. The discussion moved on to their planned lunch in Winslow the next day, and even Jeremy got the point and managed not to stick his foot in his mouth during the rest of the conversation.

After that, Jake and Addie wandered through the party, saying hello to people they hadn't seen in a while, or having him make introductions to the relatives she hadn't yet met. And yes, there were Natalie and Ethan, the two of them doing their best to mingle with all the Wilcoxes. In fact, the two of them looked downright glowing, the reason for their appearance becoming clear soon enough.

"We're expecting in early May," Ethan said proudly.

"Congratulations!" Addie and Jake responded, nearly in unison. She grinned and gave Natalie a quick hug, then added, "That's fabulous news!"

"It looks like you have some news of your own," Natalie replied with a significant glance toward the diamond on Addie's left hand. "When's your big day?"

"June sometime, we think," she said. "We haven't quite nailed it down yet."

"Well, congratulations," Ethan said. "It looks like next year is going to be a big one for all of us."

"That's for sure," Jake told him. "You've talked to Eleanor?"

"Yes," Natalie said. "But we're actually going to see the same ob/gyn who delivered all of

Connor and Angela's kids. Eleanor said that's what a lot of you Wilcoxes do."

Which was true. Eleanor had delivered quite a few babies in her time, but a lot of the younger witches in the clan preferred to see a civilian doctor. Jake wondered what Addie would want to do when it was her turn, although he told himself that day would probably be quite a while off. She hadn't said anything concrete, but he had the impression that she definitely wanted to get her master's degree and work for a few years before she started a family. And he was all right with that. To tell the truth, he preferred to have her to himself for a while before they took on the task of raising children.

"Yes, a lot of my cousins have gone to see Dr. Ruiz," he replied. "She's supposed to be amazing."

"I think so," Natalie said. One hand went to touch her stomach, which was barely rounded at that point. "At least, she's been great so far."

"Aunt Addie!" came a chorus of voices, and Jake turned to see Connor and Angela's three kids bearing down on them.

That signaled the end of the conversation, because Addie got dragged off to play on the Xbox with her nieces and nephew and some other cousins around their age. She laughed and gamely went along, although Jake made sure to stay close so he could intervene at what looked like an appropriate moment.

Eventually, though, Angela came along and rescued her, and said it was time to start lining up to eat. The game broke up as the kids scampered off to grab some paper plates and get their meals, although Angela stayed with them to make sure they didn't just load up on potatoes and dessert.

Jake was used to the amazing variety of food offered and did his best to avoid sampling everything. Addie overfilled her plate and had to appeal to him to help her finish it, but that was all right. He'd left some room because he had a feeling that very thing might happen.

It felt good, being there with her. He couldn't help contrasting this potluck with the ones Connor's older brother Damon had thrown during his tenure as *primus*. On the surface, the party didn't seem that different—a large, friendly group of well-dressed people, food everywhere, a big Christmas tree and holiday music in the background. However, a certain tension had always underlaid any get-together where the former *primus* had been present. Like his father before him, Damon hadn't been a very reassuring person. Connor's laid-back personality was pretty much the exact opposite of his brother's...and of course, Damon had never had anyone like Angela McAllister at his side.

Dusk had fallen by the time Jake and Addie left. Once again, stars burned in the black sky, relentless in revealing how utterly clear it remained. To his relief, though, she didn't seem as keyed up by the situation as he'd feared she would be. Possibly that was due to the several glasses of wine she'd drunk at the party, but he still deemed it better to remain silent than bring up a topic they'd been trying to avoid.

They appeased the dog by feeding her a few bites of turkey they'd brought home with them, then headed into the family room to put their feet up and watch some TV. Addie leaned her head on his shoulder and said, "That was good."

"The food?" he asked, even though he knew she'd probably meant something different.

"No," she replied. "I mean, yes, the food was great. Just…the party. Seeing everyone. It was fun."

"I told you we don't bite."

"Unless asked, of course."

He chuckled, then picked up her hand and pressed a gentle kiss against her palm. "I didn't know you were into the rough stuff."

"I think you know I'm not."

True. She was passionate and almost always ready to follow him to the bedroom—or to use the couch if they didn't feel like going upstairs—but she didn't seem to have any particular kinks. A relief, really, because he didn't, either. Pure vanilla, the both of them.

And that was okay.

"I'm glad you had fun," he said.

"It was a good Christmas."

But then she sighed, and he guessed she wasn't thinking about the party they'd just attended. "You don't have to worry about that tonight," he told her quietly. "It can wait."

"It can't wait forever."

"Until after tomorrow, then."

She shifted, raising her head from his shoulder so she could look him in the eyes. "I thought we were only going to wait until after Christmas."

"Well, tomorrow is Boxing Day," he pointed out. "That's basically Christmas."

"Are you going to keep making excuses for me all the way through New Year's?"

If that's what it takes, he thought, but he knew better than to say those words aloud. "No," he said. "But we already had plans with Jeremy and Sloane. One more day. That's all."

For a moment, he thought she was going to argue with him, but then her shoulders lifted, and she snuggled up against him again, head back on his shoulder. "What do you want to watch?"

That was all she said, but he understood. They'd had a wonderful day, and she didn't want to push things. Not on Christmas.

"We'll surf," he replied, and picked up the remote, figuring he could find a holiday movie they hadn't watched yet.

Once again, he thought that being with her was the very best present he could ever have.

9

Addie

SOMETIME AFTER MIDNIGHT, I OPENED MY eyes. I had no idea what might have awakened me —I tended to sleep like a log, and rarely got up in the middle of the night—but there I was, staring at the ceiling, listening to Jake breathe deeply next to me. A faint light came into the room from the nightlight in the bathroom down the hall, illuminating enough to show me that Taffy was asleep as well, curled into a little ball in her bed. A faint rattle in the vents told me the central heat was working away in the background, protecting us from the sub-freezing temperatures outside.

Very carefully, I slid my legs out from underneath the covers and stood up. Jake didn't stir, so I headed to the closet and fetched my robe and slippers. Thus protected, I padded downstairs, went into the powder room and took care of business, then made my way into the kitchen, where I poured myself a glass of water.

We'd turned off the lights on the Christmas tree when we headed upstairs for bed, and so the downstairs was dark, except for the under-cupboard lights I'd turned on when I came into the kitchen. I knew they weren't bright enough to reach all the way to the second story, and so I doubted they would wake up Jake. More likely, he'd somehow sense I was gone and come down to the kitchen to see if everything was all right.

I thought it was. Or at least, I'd survived the onslaught of the Wilcox clan's Christmas potluck without any ill effects, except maybe the realization that I'd probably eaten enough to put on a pound or two. No biggie, though. Wasn't that what the holidays were for?

So strange to be a part of this big, sprawling witch family. Some days, it still didn't quite feel real, as if I thought I'd wake up at some point and realize the handsome warlock who loved me—and my half-brother and his wife and everyone else I'd met—had only been part of some kind of super-detailed extended dream.

But no, this was my life now. I had to hope that somewhere my mother could still see me, could know that everything in my life was going well. That, against all odds, my father's family had accepted me as one of their own.

It should have been enough.

On one level, I knew it was. If someone had asked me a year earlier what my ideal life looked like, I doubted I could have dreamed up anything better than the existence I was blessed to be living. Underneath, though, was a thin thread of dissatisfaction. Not with anything in my personal life… only the uncomfortable knowledge that something was terribly wrong in the world and I didn't know how to fix it.

Part of me wanted to argue that I shouldn't have to shoulder that kind of responsibility. What I'd seen from this remarkable family of mine, though, was that they didn't shy away from tackling a problem. If their gift was the one that could fix a certain situation, then they'd do what they could to make things better. No blaming others or complaining that it wasn't fair, or that they hadn't caused the problem and shouldn't be forced to fix it.

Which meant I shouldn't be doing that, either, even if underneath it all, I was justifiably pissed off at Lori and Lisa Freeman for creating this mess in the first place.

Jake had urged me to let it go until after our trip to Winslow, but clearly, something inside me was saying it didn't want to go along with that plan. The digital clock on the stove told me that midnight had come and gone almost two hours earlier. Christmas was over, and I needed to do what I could to fix things.

Except...I had no idea exactly how I was supposed to accomplish such a feat.

I thought of the way Joanna and I had combined our powers to attack the spell and break it down. Although I still didn't know exactly what had happened, I knew the blowback had been enough to knock her unconscious, if only for a moment. Strangely, I hadn't been affected at all. What that meant, I wasn't sure. Was it simply that my weather-working powers were much stronger than hers, and therefore had managed to shield me somehow?

That explanation made about as much sense as anything else I'd been able to think of.

We'd been trying to brute-force our way past the spell. I'd imagined a wall, of removing the bricks from that wall one by one. But weather didn't really work that way. It flowed from place to place, following its own currents, its own energy. That energy had to be building and building, dammed up as it was in one place.

I had to free it. But how?

My head hurt.

I went to the refrigerator and dispensed more

water from the door. No ice, because I didn't want to risk the rattle of ice cubes in my glass. For some reason, I knew Jake needed to stay asleep. I couldn't have him interrupting me.

Weather flowed like a river. It was currently blocked and dammed by the Freeman sisters' spell, but sometimes even a dam wasn't enough to keep a river in check. If it wanted to, the water would find a way to flow around the dam, to dig a new channel for itself.

Of course.

I took the glass of water with me as I went to the back door and opened it. At once, a flood of icy air poured over me, but I ignored the chill. My heavy fleece robe and Ugg boots would protect me for long enough.

Or at least, I hoped they would.

I descended the porch steps, clearly aware of the bite of the chill breeze that moved through the yard. It seemed to burn against my cheeks, but I ignored it. Instead, I walked to the middle of the frost-yellowed lawn and stood there silently for a moment, breathing in and out, feeling the burn of the frigid air in my throat and in my lungs.

Oh, yes, it was definitely cold enough.

Hardly aware of what I was doing, I lifted the glass of water and poured out its contents, tracing an undulating shape across the dead grass. Almost at once, the water turned to ice, glinting beneath the frost-sharp stars overhead.

There is your path, I thought. *Not through, but around. Find a new flow. Find a new road to travel.*

For the longest moment, everything was dead silent. The breeze that had tugged at my loose hair stilled, as if the entire world had pulled in a breath and now held it, not knowing what to do next. I didn't dare to breathe, either. What if this didn't work? What if it made things worse?

If the unthinkable happened, I knew I wouldn't be able to fix it.

Please.

And then....

Then that blockage I'd sensed so many hundreds of miles away seemed to fragment, to shatter. It was like the nature films I'd seen in grade school, where they showed an ice sheet breaking up during the spring thaw. So many cracks, radiating outward. And underneath the shattered ice, the water flowing again, brisk and joyful, running along the new channels I'd just shown it.

The wind returned, stronger now, rustling the few dead leaves left on the trees and keening through the pines that ringed the yard. I bent my head against that wind, knowing it was stronger than I.

Since it didn't need me anymore, I made my way over to the porch and let myself into the house. At once, warm air faintly scented with the vanilla cinnamon potpourri I'd set out for the holidays surrounded me. I released a breath, letting go of the cold air that had settled in my lungs.

And I went to the window so I could look outside. The wind still blew, but the stars were as sharp and bright as ever.

But then a shadow moved over them, and another. Clouds scudding across the ebony sky, more and more of them.

One pale flake, then another. And another. Soon, snow was falling like mist, swirling in the wind, coating the bare elm branches and the pine trees alike.

I smiled.

Time to go to bed.

"Addie!"

I sat up in bed, blinking. Jake stood by the window, the blinds opened their widest to reveal billows of snow flowing past. "What?" I asked sleepily.

He pointed at the snow. "Did you do this?"

No point in denying it. "Yes."

"When?"

"Last night," I replied. "I couldn't sleep, so I went downstairs to get a drink of water. Then...I guess I sort of figured it out. The snow started to fall, and I came back to bed."

His brows lifted. "Why didn't you wake me up?"

"Because you were asleep," I said reasonably. "I figured if I really had broken the Freeman twins' spell, then the snow wasn't going anywhere."

"That's for damn sure," he replied, sounding bemused. "You should come take a look at this."

I pushed back the covers and went to the window. From her bed, Taffy blinked at me, clearly not ready to leave its warmth to brave the snowy morning.

Because it was definitely snowy. The flakes were coming down so thick that I could barely see the trees on the other side of the yard. Overnight, drifts had piled nearly two feet high, if not more.

"Well, it's not exactly Christmas," I said. "But it's definitely white."

He chuckled. "You don't do anything by halves, do you?"

About all I could do was shrug. "I don't know if this is all my doing. This is pent-up energy finally getting a chance to release itself."

"Maybe," he allowed. "But I still think you're pretty damn impressive."

He lifted my hair out of the way so he could press a kiss against the side of my neck, sending a delicious shiver through me. Somehow, he always knew the exact right place to kiss to make me want him all over again.

"I have a feeling, though," he went on, "that we're not going to make it to Winslow today."

Right. With snow piling up that quickly, no one would be going much of anywhere. Sloane and Jeremy would be disappointed, but we could reschedule. I reached out with that strange gift of mine, reading the winds. Yes, snow would fall the rest of that day and into the night, but then the storms would clear, and so would the roads. And we'd have a few days' respite before another storm came to blanket the area with even more snow.

When the hour was decent, I'd have to call the Freemans and let them know their spell was broken...and possibly hint that they really shouldn't try something like that ever again.

"No," I told Jake, then turned so I could wrap my arms around him and snuggle close to his chest, "it looks like we'll have to stay in. Whatever will we do?"

His dark eyes glinted. "I can think of a few things."

No need for words after that as he kissed me

again, then lifted me so he could carry me over to the bed. No need for anything but the two of us making our own kind of heat.

I couldn't think of anything better than that.

The Witches of Wheeler Park series will continue with Joanna's story in *Blood Ties,* releasing in February 2021.

ALSO BY CHRISTINE POPE

HEDGEWITCH FOR HIRE

(Mystery/Paranormal romance)

Grave Mistake (January 2021)

Social Medium (March 2021)

THE WITCHES OF WHEELER PARK

(Paranormal romance)

Storm Born

Thunder Road

Winds of Change

Mind Games

A Wheeler Park Christmas

Blood Ties (February 2021)

PROJECT DEMON HUNTERS*

(Paranormal Romance)

Unquiet Souls

Haunted Hearts

THE WITCHES OF CLEOPATRA HILL*

(Paranormal Romance)

Darkangel

Darknight

Darkmoon

Sympathetic Magic

Protector

Spellbound

A Cleopatra Hill Christmas

Impractical Magic

Strange Magic

The Arrangement

Defender

Bad Blood

Deep Magic

Darktide

THE DJINN WARS*

(Paranormal Romance)

Chosen

Taken

Fallen

Broken

Forsaken

Forbidden

Awoken

Illuminated

Stolen

Forgotten

Driven

Unspoken

THE WATCHERS TRILOGY*

(Paranormal Romance)

Falling Dark

Dead of Night

Rising Dawn

THE SEDONA FILES*

(Paranormal Romance)

Bad Vibrations

Desert Hearts

Angel Fire

Star Crossed

Falling Angels

Enemy Mine

TALES OF THE LATTER KINGDOMS*

(Fantasy Romance)

All Fall Down

Dragon Rose

Binding Spell

Ashes of Roses

One Thousand Nights

Threads of Gold

The Wolf of Harrow Hall

Moon Dance

The Song of the Thrush

THE GAIAN CONSORTIUM SERIES*

(Science Fiction Romance)

Beast (free prequel novella)

Blood Will Tell

Breath of Life

The Gaia Gambit

The Mandala Maneuver

The Titan Trap

The Zhore Deception

The Refugee Ruse

STANDALONE TITLES

Hearts on Fire

Taking Dictation

Golden Heart

Night Music: A Modern Reimagining of The Phantom of the Opera

Ghost Dance: A Sequel to Gaston Leroux's The Phantom of the Opera

* Indicates a completed series

ABOUT THE AUTHOR

USA Today bestselling author Christine Pope has been writing stories ever since she commandeered her family's Smith-Corona typewriter back in grade school. Her work includes paranormal romance, fantasy romance, and science fiction/space opera romance. She makes her home in Arizona's beautiful Verde Valley.

Christine Pope on the Web:
www.christinepope.com

 facebook.com/ChristinePopeAuthor

 twitter.com/ChristineJPope

 pinterest.com/ChristineJPope